Look for the first Manor House Mystery . . .
A Bicycle Built for Murder

MORE MYSTERIES FROM THE
BERKLEY PUBLISHING GROUP...

SISTER FREVISSE MYSTERIES: Medieval mystery in the tradition of Ellis Peters . . .

by Margaret Frazer

THE NOVICE'S TALE   THE BISHOP'S TALE   THE REEVE'S TALE
THE OUTLAW'S TALE   THE BOY'S TALE   THE SQUIRE'S TALE
THE PRIORESS' TALE   THE MURDERER'S TALE
THE SERVANT'S TALE   THE MAIDEN'S TALE

PENNYFOOT HOTEL MYSTERIES: In Edwardian England, death takes a seaside holiday . . .

by Kate Kingsbury

ROOM WITH A CLUE   DO NOT DISTURB   CHIVALRY IS DEAD
SERVICE FOR TWO   EAT, DRINK, AND BE BURIED RING FOR TOMB SERVICE
CHECK-OUT TIME   GROUNDS FOR MURDER   MAID TO MURDER
DEATH WITH RESERVATIONS   PAY THE PIPER

GLYNIS TRYON MYSTERIES: The highly acclaimed series set in the early days of the women's rights movement . . . "Historically accurate and telling."—Sara Paretsky

by Miriam Grace Monfredo

SENECA FALLS INHERITANCE   THROUGH A GOLD EAGLE   MUST THE MAIDEN DIE
BLACKWATER SPIRITS   THE STALKING-HORSE   SISTERS OF CAIN
NORTH STAR CONSPIRACY

MARK TWAIN MYSTERIES: "Adventurous . . . Replete with genuine tall tales from the great man himself."—*Mostly Murder*

by Peter J. Heck

DEATH ON THE MISSISSIPPI
A CONNECTICUT YANKEE IN CRIMINAL COURT   THE GUILTY ABROAD
THE PRINCE AND THE PROSECUTOR   THE MYSTERIOUS STRANGLER

KAREN ROSE CERCONE: A stunning new historical mystery series featuring Detective Milo Kachigan and social worker Helen Sorby . . .

STEEL ASHES   BLOOD TRACKS   COAL BONES

Death Is in the Air

KATE KINGSBURY

BERKLEY PRIME CRIME, NEW YORK

This is a work of fiction. Names, characters, places, and incidents are either the product of the author's imagination or are used fictitiously, and any resemblance to actual persons, living or dead, business establishments, events, or locales is entirely coincidental.

DEATH IS IN THE AIR

A Berkley Prime Crime Book / published by arrangement with the author

PRINTING HISTORY
Berkley Prime Crime edition / August 2001

Visit our website at
www.penguinputnam.com

ISBN: 0-425-18094-8

Berkley Prime Crime Books are published
by The Berkley Publishing Group,
a division of Penguin Putnam Inc.,
375 Hudson Street, New York, New York 10014.
The name BERKLEY PRIME CRIME and the BERKLEY PRIME
CRIME design
are trademarks belonging to Penguin Putnam Inc.

PRINTED IN THE UNITED STATES OF AMERICA

10 9 8 7 6 5 4 3 2 1

ACKNOWLEDGMENTS

Grateful thanks to my wonderful editor, Judith Palais, without whose guidance and encouragement this series would not exist. Thank you for making me look good.

My thanks also to Ann Wraight, a resident of England and lifetime friend, for keeping the memories alive, and for supplying me with useful research material.

And to Bill, for being my best friend as well as my devoted husband. I could not do this without you.

CHAPTER

❧ 1 ❧

Lady Elizabeth Hartleigh Compton rarely visited the hairdresser's. Normally she had Marlene Barnett come to the Manor House to tend to her hair, which grew uncommonly fast and was inclined to rage out of control whenever she rode her motorcycle into the village.

That morning, however, she'd been seized with an uncontrollable urge to have her hair trimmed immediately. When she'd called Marlene to make an appointment, the young woman had been most apologetic. Two of the hairdressers were home with a cold, and she was just too busy to come to the Manor House. Perhaps next week?

At first Elizabeth had considered asking her housekeeper to give her a trim. Violet made no secret of the fact that she cut her own hair, and at times had wielded a pair of scissors above the head of Martin, Elizabeth's aging butler, even though Martin had less than a dozen wisps to worry about.

Envisioning the way Violet's frizzy gray mop sprouted from her head like a much-used scouring pad, Elizabeth had reluctantly accepted Marlene's polite suggestion that she come down to the shop where she'd do her best to fit her in.

Seated in front of a badly speckled mirror, almost suffocated by a cloud of cigarette smoke, Elizabeth wondered why she'd been in such a hurry to get her hair cut. It was most inconvenient for the hairdressers to catch colds this early in September.

The peculiar chemical smell that pervaded the shop was revolting, and she wasn't too thrilled about being drawn into the gossip being avidly exchanged between the rest of the customers. Especially since the most strident of the voices belonged to her archenemy, Rita Crumm.

Rita had always made her voice heard in the tiny village of Sitting Marsh. Since the advent of the Second World War, however, Rita had come into her own. She had made the war effort her own personal crusade and had rounded up enough gullible followers among the housewives in the village to form a sizable group, most of whom followed her orders with ill-advised enthusiasm.

Elizabeth was well aware that Rita was more intent on basking in the glory of her supervision than of actually achieving any worthwhile war effort. Not only that, she was using her self-appointed position of authority to usurp the lady of the manor, whom she considered unworthy of the title. It was no secret in Sitting Marsh that Elizabeth's mother had been a kitchen maid until she'd caught the eye of the Earl of Wellsborough and married him. Adding fuel to the flames was the fact that Sitting Marsh's new landlady belonged to that much maligned species, the divorcée.

Elizabeth winced as Rita's harsh tones effectively cut

off the voice of the timid woman seated next to her. "Did you hear about the big fight down at the Tudor Arms last night? Alfie said they broke dozens of bottles and glasses. It's a wonder someone didn't get really hurt. Bloody Yanks should go back where they came from, that's what I say."

Marlene wound Rita's mousy brown hair around the last metal curler and securely fastened it. "I don't know why everyone complains about the Yanks so much. Now that they've taken over the airdrome here, there's been more money spent in the village than in all the years I've been around. Look at the business Ted Wilkins is doing down at the pub! I bet he's not complaining about the Yanks. The Tudor Arms never had it so good."

Rita glared at the brazen hussy who'd dared to contradict her. "The money's not doing Ted much good if he has to pay for the damage them Yanks do while they're busy punching our army boys instead of the Germans."

"I wouldn't mind betting our boys started it. They're blooming jealous of the Yanks, that's why." Marlene moved over to Elizabeth's chair and draped an evil-smelling green cape around her shoulders. "Them Yanks have all the money and all the glamour, don't they. No wonder all the girls are flocking around them. They make the British blokes look like pansies."

"I noticed you haven't wasted any time getting to know some of them," Rita said, coloring her comment with a loud sniff.

Marlene grinned. "Of course I haven't. I'd be really stupid not to go after them. They know how to treat a girl, don't they?"

"Well, all I can say is, they should know how to keep themselves to themselves." Rita sent a sly glance in Elizabeth's direction. "Of course, that's a little hard to do when some people are taking them into their own homes."

Elizabeth tightened her lips. She'd held her tongue for

the last half hour. Her mother would have been proud
of her. Her mother had always maintained that a still
tongue dwells in a wise head. But conscious of the
sheepish glances being sent her way, she felt compelled
to defend herself against Rita's criticism.

"It is somewhat difficult to refuse a direct request
from the government to provide quarters for the American officers. One can hardly turn down the Ministry of
War at a time like this, and after all, I have plenty of
room at the manor. I'm happy to do what I can for the
war effort."

At the mention of the war effort, Rita's chin shot up.
Those words were like a trumpet call to her ears. "Well,
we all have to do what we can these days, I'm sure.
Though some of us have to make *real* sacrifices."

Elizabeth felt her blood heating up at the well-aimed
barb, but before she could respond, the thin droning of
an airplane made itself heard above the clatter in the
shop. Everyone fell silent. Even Rita ceased her chatter
to listen.

"One of ours?" one of the women asked fearfully.

"Hard to tell." Marlene walked over to the door.
"Whatever it is, it sounds as if it's in trouble." The spluttering sound of an engine confirmed her observation.

Rita got up from her chair, and, like sheep, the other
four women followed. Marching in line wearing their
helmets of metal curlers, they looked for all the world
like ancient soldiers heading into battle. Elizabeth
watched them all in the mirror as the spluttering grew
more pronounced.

Marlene opened the door and stepped into the street.
As she did so, one of the women uttered a loud shriek.
"My God, it's a bloody Nazi! There's a swastika on its
tail!"

"Inside, everybody!" Rita yelled. "Take cover! We're
being invaded!"

"I don't think so," Marlene said, staring skyward. "I
think the poor bugger's trying to land."

Her words galvanized Elizabeth into action. Thrusting aside the green cape, she leapt from her chair and rushed to the door. The rest of the women charged in the opposite direction, nearly sweeping her off her feet in their hurry to find shelter.

Joining Marlene on the pavement outside, Elizabeth shaded her eyes against the bright sunlight as she followed the young girl's transfixed gaze. The plane was indeed a German bomber, longer than a Messerschmitt, but with the distinctive black German cross on each wing. Her stomach heaved. Her parents had been killed in London during the Blitz. Probably by bombs from a plane like this one.

In spite of the danger, she felt compelled to watch the plane dip lower as the engine coughed and spluttered again, then died altogether. The bomber seemed to be coming right at her, yet her legs refused to move. She felt as if her entire body had turned to ice.

She felt Marlene tug on her arm, heard her screaming something, yet she was powerless to turn away from the awesome sight of the plane drifting silently now above the roofs of the shops along the High Street in the direction of the ocean. Then she saw why Marlene was still pointing at the sky after the bomber had passed over. Floating gently down to earth was the white silky mushroom of a parachute.

The man dangling beneath it swayed to and fro in the sea breeze. Marlene jumped up and down at Elizabeth's side, still grasping her arm—something she would never do under normal circumstances. A commoner never actually touched the lady of the manor unless it was a matter of life and death. *Which it could very well be*, Elizabeth thought with remarkable composure as she watched the enemy pilot falling more rapidly now as he neared the ground.

"The silly sod's going to land on the village green!" Marlene yelled.

At the sound of her words, bedlam erupted inside the

hairdresser's shop. Rita's booming voice rang out in an attempt to restore order as the women bolted into the street. "Wait, you blithering idiots! We have to capture the prisoner!"

"You bloody capture him!" one woman yelled. "I'm going home and locking myself inside."

"Rita's right," Elizabeth called out, suddenly coming to life. "We can't let him get away. Get everyone out in the street!" Even as she shouted the words, she could see people spilling out from the shops.

Jack Mitchem rushed out of his butcher's shop carrying a wicked-looking knife, followed closely by Harold, the greengrocer from next door, who brandished a shovel.

Afraid now that they'd kill the German, Elizabeth started running toward the green. She heard a dull explosion in the distance and guessed the plane had landed on the beach, no doubt on a landmine. The beaches were covered with them in case of an invasion.

The pilot was on the ground now and trying to disentangle himself from the ropes of his parachute. He lifted his head as she drew closer, and she halted.

The German finally freed himself and pulled his flying helmet from his head. Then, to her utter relief, he dropped the helmet on the ground and raised his hands in obvious surrender.

Somewhat subdued, the crowd gathered around the green, encircling the man. Everyone looked at Elizabeth. Even Rita Crumm looked flustered, and she hung back as if waiting for someone to tell her what to do.

Elizabeth drew in a deep breath. Clearly the next move was up to her. As lady of the manor, she was responsible for the welfare of these people. She was in charge until the police arrived. "Someone send for the constables," she said, keeping her voice calm so as not to alarm the German.

He looked very young and very unsure of himself. She could see his hands shaking as he held them in the air. She just hoped P.C. Dalrymple would arrive on the scene shortly. Already the women were beginning to mutter behind her. Heaven knows what would happen if Rita Crumm took it into her head to lead a charge of her housewives against the poor man.

Marlene arrived at her side at that moment. "He doesn't look very dangerous," she said, running her fingers through her impressive mane of red hair. "He's rather good-looking, actually. I always did fancy blond men."

"You wouldn't think so if he was trying to stick a bayonet in your belly," Jack Mitchem growled.

"Wonder what happened to the rest of his crew," Harold muttered.

"They're probably either dead and went down with the plane, or they bailed out earlier on."

"Gawd, the whole village could be swarming with bloody Nazis."

Jack raised his knife. "I say we cut those ropes off that parachute and tie him up till George gets here."

Elizabeth thought that was a good idea. She was just about to say so when Marlene exclaimed, "Look at that parachute! All that lovely silk going to waste."

Rita's voice rose sharply from behind her. "Silk? That's real silk?"

"Too right it is." Marlene took a step forward. "That would make a lovely wedding dress."

"And petticoats," Rita murmured.

"Blouses!" someone else cried.

"Nightdresses!"

"Sheets!"

"Here, it was my idea!" Marlene darted toward the pilot, apparently intent on gathering up the parachute. Just as intent on getting their share, a dozen or more women raced behind her. The German pilot shrieked once then disappeared from view as the women scrambled around him.

"Wait!" Elizabeth called out. "Wait until George gets here. Someone could get hurt."

Her pleas went unnoticed as more women joined the throng, all squabbling and tearing at the silky folds of the parachute. Elizabeth looked down the hill and saw George pedaling his bike furiously up the slope toward her. Help was on the way.

It took the combined efforts of herself and the two men in the crowd to separate the women and restore order. When it was over there was nothing left of the parachute except a few tangled ropes. Unfortunately, there was no sign of the German pilot either. Apparently he had taken advantage of the confusion and made good his escape.

"Goodness!" Violet exclaimed after listening to Elizabeth's breathless account of the incident. "I heard on the radio that German planes fly over now and then, but I never thought I'd see one land in Sitting Marsh."

"It didn't exactly land," Elizabeth said. Seated at the ancient table in the kitchen of the Manor House, she took comfort in the cup of tea Violet had poured for her. Her hands still shook from all the excitement as she replaced her cup in its saucer. "It was more of a crash landing, and I think it blew up on the beach."

Violet carried her own cup over to the table and sat down opposite her. "I heard the explosion, but I thought it was a seagull landing on a mine. Where do you think the German went, then?"

"I have no idea, but I think if it were me I'd have made a beeline for the woods. Goodness, is that the time? I had no idea it was so late."

Violet followed her gaze to the mantelpiece clock above the huge fireplace that had once housed an oven and had served as the only means of cooking meals. The Manor House had been built early in the seventeenth century, and except for the addition of modern plumbing and electricity, remained much the same as it had been for three centuries. The kitchen, with its huge bay windows and warm brick walls, was one of Elizabeth's favorite rooms.

"I was getting quite worried about you." Violet gave her a critical stare. "I told you not to go down to that shop. You should have waited for Marlene to come up here."

Elizabeth patted her hair. "I was beginning to look straggly."

"Looked fine to me." Violet got up from the table and picked up the cups and saucers. "Did you get it cut after all that?"

Elizabeth frowned. "Can't you tell?"

"Not really. I could have done a better job than that."

"No doubt you could, but I didn't want to bother you. Now that you have all this extra work with the American officers moving into the east wing, you have your hands full." It was a good excuse, and one Elizabeth felt comfortable using. To her relief, Violet seemed pacified by her words.

"Oh, it's not that bad," she said, dismissing the suggestion with a wave of her hand. "Polly has been working pretty hard."

Elizabeth looked at her in surprise. Usually Violet didn't have a good word to say about the young housemaid. "Polly? I'm happy to hear that."

Violet nodded. "Surprised me, too. Don't know what's got into her, rushing up and down stairs and in and out of rooms like a squirrel hunting nuts. She was finished in half the time it usually took her to do the job before the Yanks moved in. Maybe she's trying to impress them."

"That wouldn't surprise me." Elizabeth reached for the pile of letters sitting on the sideboard where Martin always placed them for her. "You know she wanted to help me out in the office as well."

"So she told me." Violet placed the cups in the sink and ran hot water over them. "If you ask me, you'd be daft to let her in there. Gawd knows the damage she'd do. Not exactly that bright, our Polly."

Elizabeth merely nodded. Her mind was on the subject she wanted to broach and how to word it without upsetting Violet. Absently sifting through the bills, she said carefully, "I've decided it might be a good idea to invite Major Monroe to dinner tomorrow night. I thought we could have it in the main dining room. What do you think?"

Violet spun around to face her. "So that's why you got your hair cut."

Elizabeth could feel her cheeks growing warm. "Don't be silly, Violet."

"You're the one being silly. I thought you said you wouldn't be caught dead with a Yank?"

Elizabeth lifted her chin. Violet had been with the family since she was born. After Lord and Lady Hartleigh had perished in a bombing raid while attending a concert in London, Violet had done her best to fill in, and it had been largely due to her efforts that Elizabeth had succeeded in taking over the reigns of the Manor House and its huge estate. Nevertheless, there was a limit to which she would allow the housekeeper's interference in her personal life, no matter how well meaning.

In fact, Elizabeth was well aware that if her mother were able to witness the familiarity between her only heir and a lowly servant, she would come back to haunt both of them. Mavis Hartleigh had spent the major portion of her life trying to live down the fact that until she'd married the future Earl of Wellsborough, she'd been a servant herself.

"Violet," Elizabeth said, fixing a stern eye on Violet's pinched features. "Any interest I might have in Major Monroe is strictly business. He is in command of the men billeted in this house, and there are certain concerns that should be addressed. I merely thought it might be more pleasant to share a meal while discussing our business, rather than the stuffy atmosphere of the library or my office. It would be more conducive for an honest exchange of views, don't you think?"

"I've seen the way you look when his name is mentioned," Violet retorted, refusing to be intimidated. "Don't tell me you don't feel a spark of something when he's around."

Elizabeth pursed her lips. Wild horses wouldn't drag that admission from her, no matter how close to the mark it might have been. "Major Monroe is married," she said primly.

"Go on!" Violet rushed over to the table and sat down. "When did he tell you that?"

Elizabeth stared hard at the bills in her hand. "I really don't remember. It came up some time in one of our conversations."

"Bet that was a disappointment."

That was something else she wasn't prepared to admit. Instead, Elizabeth held up a letter. "Look at this! It's a letter from Uncle Roger."

Violet's expression changed to one of contempt. "What's he want now?"

Elizabeth tore open the envelope, more relieved at the diversion than interest in the letter. She scanned the lines then refolded the flimsy paper. "He's got a spot of leave coming up and wants to pay us a visit."

"Probably on the earhole for money or something. We never see him unless he wants something. If I had my way I wouldn't let him past the front door."

"If you had your way," Elizabeth murmured, "no one would get past the front door."

Violet opened her mouth to answer then snapped it shut as the door to the kitchen flew open.

The elderly gentleman standing in the doorway wore the black coat and gray striped trousers of the traditional, efficient English butler, but there the image ended. Gold-rimmed spectacles hung precariously on the end of his nose, and the few wisps of white hair that adorned his bald pate waved back and forth as his head nodded up and down in gentle agitation. His bowed shoulders shook, and his knees trembled as he stared at Elizabeth, and without a sound his mouth opened and closed like a starving goldfish.

Alarmed, Elizabeth rose from her chair. Martin had served the Earls of Wellsborough since before the turn of the century. Determined that he should continue to do so as long as he so desired, she and Violet went to great pains to convince him his services were still essential to the running of the Manor House.

She largely ignored his occasional lapses into senility as well as his tendency to dwell in the past, but looking at his stricken face, seemingly even more wrinkled and pasty than usual, Elizabeth sensed that whatever had caused his distress this time was more than a simple misunderstanding, which was often the case.

Martin had been unsettled by the American officers being quartered at the Manor House, but since he saw little of them and was largely oblivious to their presence, he'd appeared to accept the situation. Nevertheless, something had upset the old gentleman.

Stepping up to him, Elizabeth laid a hand on his frail shoulder. "Martin? What is it?"

Martin shuddered beneath her fingers. He finally spoke, and his voice sounded as dry and cracked as burned leather. "The master," he whispered. "I saw him in the great hall."

"That's nonsense," Violet snapped, apparently unsettled herself by the old man's obvious distress. "You know very well, Martin, that Lord Hartleigh passed away two years ago. You put flowers on his grave just last week."

Martin drew himself up as straight as was physically possible, and his voice regained strength as he stared at Violet. "His body may be buried in that grave," he said hoarsely, "but I just saw his ghost walking down the great hall. I'd stake my life on it."

CHAPTER

🙞 2 🙜

"Didn't sleep a wink last night," Violet declared the next morning when Elizabeth walked into the kitchen. "What with that German bomber pilot on the loose somewhere and Martin's ghost, I was afraid to shut my eyes."

"What ghost?" Polly demanded, withdrawing her head from the broom closet.

Violet made a sound of disgust. "Mind your manners, Polly. Say good morning to madam."

Polly gave Elizabeth a cheeky grin. "Oops, sorry. Morning, m'm."

Elizabeth returned the greeting. "I wouldn't pay too much attention to Martin. You know how he is." She accepted the cup of tea Violet handed her and sat down at the table.

"He did seem really upset, all the same." Violet turned back to the stove. "Even for him."

"He probably saw one of the Yanks wandering

around," Polly said, hauling her bucket and mop over to the door. "Though I haven't seem much of them since they've been here."

She disappeared, and Violet shook her head. "Thank Gawd for that. I don't trust them Yanks. Nor Polly for that matter."

Martin had placed the weekly local newspaper next to Elizabeth's table mat, and she picked it up. "You worry too much Violet," she murmured.

"Someone around here has to," Violet muttered darkly.

Elizabeth stopped listening to her, her attention caught by the thick black headlines stamped across the front page. *German Pilot Escapes!* they screamed, and in smaller letters, *Dangerous Enemy on the Loose in Hawthorn Woods!*

According to the news report, soldiers from the camp in nearby Beerstowe had joined the local constabulary in a manhunt, and residents of the village were warned to stay away from the woods, where the pilot was suspected of having gone to ground.

Aware that Violet was talking to her, Elizabeth tore her gaze from the newspaper. "I beg your pardon?"

Violet crossed her arms. "I was asking if you and your major will be having dinner in the dining room tonight. What's in that paper that's so interesting, anyway?"

Elizabeth read the report out loud. "I feel sorry for the poor man," she said when she was finished. "He looked so young, hardly more than a boy, and he was obviously terrified."

"I should think so. I'd be terrified, too, if I saw Rita Crumm and her mob rushing at me. Enough to scare Hitler hisself, that woman." Violet tilted her head to one side. "You never answered me about your major."

"He's not my major, Violet." Elizabeth folded the newspaper and laid it next to her knife. "And I'd appreciate it if you would stop calling him that. You know how impressionable Polly is—I really don't want any silly gossip going around. Especially now that Major Monroe is staying at the manor."

Violet nodded. "So is he coming to dinner or not?"

"I haven't asked him yet."

"Well, would you mind getting on with it? That's where you should be eating your meals, anyway. It isn't proper for a lady of the manor to be taking her meals with the servants in the kitchen."

Elizabeth sighed at the familiar argument. "You know very well how much I hate eating all alone at that enormous table in the dining room. Besides, as you also know very well, I don't think of you and Martin as servants. I consider you both family."

Violet's cheeks turned pink. "That's lovely, Lizzie, but your mother wouldn't like that."

"She wouldn't like you calling me Lizzie, either, but since she's not here, and I am, I think we can stop worrying about her approval and just do what we think is right."

"If you say so." Violet looked inordinately pleased. "Now, about dinner tonight. I need to know what to buy at the butcher's this morning. Thank goodness we still have enough coupons left in the ration books for a decent meal."

Elizabeth glanced at the clock on the mantelpiece. "I'll try to catch the major before he leaves for the base. They all came back late last night, and I didn't like to ask him then."

"I know, I heard them. Them bloody water pipes were making such a racket I wonder they didn't wake the dead. No wonder poor old Martin thought he saw a ghost."

"I suppose we really should get them seen to, now that Major Monroe's men are using the east wing bathroom. I didn't think anyone would be using it again after Mummy and Daddy died."

"Maybe your major could ask one of his men to take a look at the pipes."

"He's not—" Elizabeth began, but Violet interrupted her.

"I know, he's not your major. Ask him anyway. Here's your porridge. Eat it while it's hot." She dumped a steaming plate of creamed oatmeal in front of Elizabeth.

"I'm sure the American officers have enough to do defending our skies against German bombers." Elizabeth picked up her spoon. "We'll have to find someone ourselves."

"Then you'll have to go into North Horsham to find a plumber. There are precious few men left in Sitting Marsh, and not one of them would know how to fix a water pipe."

Violet was right, Elizabeth thought gloomily. Most of the men in the village had been called up or had volunteered for the forces, and those who were left were either too old or too busy with their own businesses to help out with anything short of an emergency.

Her gaze wandered to the newspaper headlines again. The only constabulary left in Sitting Marsh were two elderly men dragged out of retirement to replace those who had joined up to fight for their country. George and Sid did their best, but apprehending a desperate enemy pilot went far beyond their meager capabilities. She could only hope the army routed out the man quickly, before panic spread among the villagers.

She had almost finished her porridge when the telephone jangled loudly across the kitchen, making Violet drop the saucepan she was drying onto the tiled kitchen counter.

"Blasted telephone," Violet grumbled as she reached for it. "I wish there was some way we could turn down the noise it makes. I jump every time it rings." She held the receiver to her ear. "Hello?"

Elizabeth watched her face for some clue as to who might be ringing at this early hour. To her dismay, she heard Violet gasp. "Go on! No, I don't believe it. Yes, of course I'll tell her. Oh, my Gawd, what dreadful news!"

On her feet now, Elizabeth stared at Violet as she replaced the receiver and turned slowly to face her. All kinds of scenarios raced through her mind . . . the uppermost being the possibility that the Germans had launched the long-expected invasion. She waited, afraid to ask the question that hovered on her lips.

"You're never going to believe this," Violet said hoarsely, "but that was Marlene. She wanted to warn Polly. That scared young German pilot you felt so sorry for has gone and killed one of the land girls from Macclesby's farm. They just found her dead body in Hawthorn Woods."

Polly sat back on her heels and wiped the sweat from her brow. Scrubbing bathrooms was the thing she hated most about her job. She often wondered why she didn't pack it in and go down to the canning factory. From what the other girls said, working there was a lot of fun. 'Course, she'd have to lie about her age. You had to be seventeen to work at the factory, and she was only fifteen. But then she was used to lying about her age. She'd been doing it for almost two years down at the pub, and only last week she'd lied to that nice Yank she'd met. Told him she was twenty. He'd believed her, too.

Polly smiled as she wrung out her mop. Goodlooking, that Sam. Had to be at least twenty-four. Stolen her heart right away he had, with his dark-brown bedroom eyes and that thick, black, curly hair. Proper man all right. She'd had to lie about her job, too. She didn't want him thinking she was just a crummy servant. She'd told him she was Lady Elizabeth's secretary. Good job he couldn't see her now, on her knees scrubbing the loo.

She leaned forward again and swiped the washrag around the pedestal of the toilet bowl. One day, she promised herself fiercely, she'd be living like a lady, too, with a secretary and a housekeeper and a butler to open the door. Only her butler would have a lot more gumption than wheezy old Martin, she'd make sure of that.

The sound of male laughter drifted down the hallway, freezing her hand. Yanks. So far she hadn't seen so much as a glimpse of Sam since he'd moved in with the others a week ago.

She'd been shocked to find out he was one of the officers billeted at the manor. Marlene had warned her that once Sam found out how she'd been lying to him, he'd never speak to her again. Marlene thought she knew everything, just because she was her older sister. Well, Polly told herself as she quickly gathered up her mop and bucket, Sam wasn't going to find out she'd been lying. She'd managed to keep out of sight of the Yanks for a week now, and she'd go on doing it as long as she had a chance with the most gorgeous man she'd ever set eyes on. And like she told Marlene, she'd keep on lying to him until he was so madly in love with her he wouldn't care when she finally told him the truth.

The voices drew closer, and before the men could round the corner she slipped out of the bathroom and through the door that led to the back stairs.

Elizabeth stared at Violet in disbelief. "That young boy killed someone? Are you sure?"

Violet shrugged. "That's what Marlene said. He cut her head wide open, Marlene said. Told me to warn Polly not to ride her bike home past the woods tonight."

"I can't believe it. He seemed so harmless."

"He wasn't bloody harmless when he was dropping them bombs over London, now was he?"

Elizabeth shook her head. "I know what you're saying, Violet, and I really can't explain how I feel. I suppose it's the fact that the young man was following orders when he dropped those bombs. Killing an innocent young woman in cold blood is something else entirely."

"Once a killer always a killer, that's what I say. Those

Germans are all alike." Violet picked up the saucepan and began scrubbing the inside of it with a scouring pad. "I should have thought you of all people would know that, seeing as how your own parents died."

Elizabeth stared at the remains of her porridge. Her appetite had disappeared, and she had no interest in cleaning up the bowl. It was hard to explain, even to herself, her sympathy toward the young German pilot.

Like everyone else, her image of a German bomber pilot was a vicious monster with hideous features hidden beneath the goggles and mask of his flying helmet. The young man standing shivering on the village green the day before was so far removed from that picture Elizabeth found it hard to believe he could actually fly a plane, let alone be responsible for dropping bombs on innocent women and children.

"I'm going to ring George Dalrymple," she announced, getting up from the table. "You know how gossip gets distorted, especially after news has been passed around that hairdresser's shop."

Violet didn't answer her, but Elizabeth could tell she didn't approve by the way she banged the saucepan down on the draining board.

There was no answer from the police station in the village, and Elizabeth hung up the telephone. "I think I'll take a run down there," she announced.

"Now, Lizzie, don't you get yourself involved in all this. Remember what happened the last time you started messing around with the murder of that poor Beryl Pierce. Almost got yourself killed, you did."

"Violet," Elizabeth said reasonably, "you know very well I was never in any real danger. In any case, I'm not getting involved. I'm merely going down to the police station to find out the truth of the matter. If indeed there is a killer on the loose in our woods, I want to know about it. Arrangements will have to be made to take Polly home tonight."

"Perhaps your major will run her home in his Jeep," Violet said, giving her a sly look.

"He's not my major." Elizabeth pulled her cardigan from the back of the chair and slipped it on. "I'll let you break the bad news to Polly. I'll be back as soon as I can."

"So what am I going to do about dinner?"

"Buy the meat. If the major can't join me, it will keep overnight in the larder. It's getting quite cool at night now."

"All right. But I'd hate to waste good meat. If he doesn't come by tomorrow night, we'll have to eat it all ourselves."

"We can always make sandwiches for the Americans."

Elizabeth almost laughed at Violet's dour expression. She might have done so if her mind wasn't still on a frightened young man hiding in the woods in fear of his life. Somewhere a mother was anxiously waiting, not knowing if her son was dead or alive. That was the trouble with war; the innocent on both sides suffered.

Martin met her in the upper hallway and peered at her above the thin gold rims of his glasses. Ever since he'd first worn the spectacles several years ago, Elizabeth had never seen him look through them. "Are you leaving, madam, or returning home?"

"I'm leaving, Martin. You didn't happen to have seen Major Monroe about this morning, I suppose?"

The wrinkles on Martin's crumpled face deepened. "Major? I don't remember ever seeing a major about here. You don't mean that scoundrel, Colonel Hartleigh, do you? He's not here, I hope." Martin's head swiveled from side to side.

"No, no, I don't mean Uncle Roger. I meant the American major. Have you seen any of the Americans?"

Martin drew himself up as straight as his spine would allow. "No, madam. Nor do I care to see them." He raised his hand and placed it over his mouth, then whispered around it, "They are the reason he came back, you know."

Elizabeth frowned. Martin's remarks often didn't make sense. Nevertheless, she hated to ignore them just in case he was trying to say something important. "Who came back?"

"Your father. I saw him as clearly as I can see you. He doesn't like these foreigners in his house. That's what he's trying to tell us."

The sounds of muffled engines caught Elizabeth's attention, and she instantly forgot about Martin's ghost. She reached for the massive door handle, but Martin uttered an exclamation and shuffled forward.

"Please, allow me, madam."

Elizabeth forced herself to wait until he grabbed hold of the handle with both hands and slowly tugged the door open. She could hear the slamming of doors outside and guessed the Americans were about to leave. If she hurried, she might just catch Major Monroe before he left.

The gap between the front door and the frame widened, and she squeezed herself through, earning a look of reproof from Martin.

"I say, madam!" he protested.

"Sorry, Martin, but I'm in a bit of hurry. Don't close the door for a moment. I won't be but a jiff." She sped down the white marble steps and across to the courtyard, where a Jeep was already rolling across the gravel to the long, curving driveway.

The young men saluted her as she rushed by, and she returned the greeting with a cheerful wave of her hand. One Jeep stood alone in the shadows of the ancient walls, engine revving as the man behind the wheel prepared to pull out.

To Elizabeth's relief, she recognized the rugged features of Major Monroe. Hurrying forward, she called out to him. "Major? I wonder if I could have a moment?"

He turned his gaze on her, and as always she felt a

quiver deep inside when she confronted his steel-blue eyes. "Ma'am?"

She felt awkward looking into that penetrating gaze and instead concentrated on the doors of the stables behind him. "I was wondering, Major, if you would care to have dinner with me tonight, here at the manor. There are several things I'd like to discuss with you, and I thought you might enjoy some home cooking for once, since you're always eating at the base and that must get really tiresome, although Violet isn't exactly a gourmet chef—actually she's not even a very good chef—but she does her best, and it should be a fairly decent meal, that's if—"

"Ma'am?"

Relieved to have an excuse to draw breath, Elizabeth returned her gaze to Major Monroe's face and found amusement dancing in his eyes.

"I'd be delighted to have dinner with you, Lady Elizabeth, and I'd enjoy sampling Violet's home cooking. On two conditions."

She eyed him warily. "All right. What are they?"

"One, this would be an informal dinner, and two, you stop calling me Major and start calling me Earl."

She would dearly love to call him by his Christian name, but somehow when she tried, the name seemed to stick in her throat. Maybe because she had never known anyone called Earl before, and it seemed so odd to give a commoner, and an American yet, a title of nobility. After all, she was the daughter of an earl, and one did not take that lightly.

If she were truly honest with herself, however, she'd be forced to admit that the reason she had so much difficulty referring to him by his first name was the air of familiarity such a procedure evoked. Though she'd die rather than admit it, Major Earl Monroe of the United States Army Air Force was far too attractive to risk sharing the least bit of familiarity.

Besides, the man was married. Which was none of

her concern, of course, but it did sort of rule out any prospects she might have been entertaining. Which she wasn't, of course.

"If it takes that long to make up your mind, perhaps we should make it some other time."

Startled, she glanced at his face but couldn't really tell from his expression if he was teasing or not. "No, of course not. I would prefer an informal meal. Actually, we can't do much else with the little rations we're allowed."

"Well, perhaps I can help out with that. I might be able to rustle up some steaks."

Aghast, she hurried to reassure him. "Oh, no, I wouldn't dream of it." She had already compromised her convictions by accepting a bottle of sherry from him. Accepting gifts from the Americans made her feel as if she were accepting charity, even though she knew that was not the intention.

Since her ex-husband's gambling habits had left her without her inheritance and deeply in debt, she was overly sensitive to anything that smacked of a donation. The Hartleighs had always fended for themselves over the centuries, and she was not about to break the tradition now.

"I guess the name thing is not going to happen, either."

On the defensive now, she lifted her chin. "I've already explained our customs to you, Major. I don't feel we know each other well enough to be on a first-name basis."

He grinned. "Well, maybe we can remedy that tonight over dinner. What time?"

The remark had been perfectly innocent. Nevertheless, she was so flustered, she stuttered. "S-s-seven o'clock?"

He glanced at the door as three of the officers strolled out into the sunlight and headed their way. "I'll be there," he said and touched the peak of his cap, managing to make the polite gesture seem incredibly intimate.

She was already regretting the invitation as she watched the Jeep roar down the tree-lined driveway and disappear around the bend. In the first place, she didn't particularly care for the sensations she experienced every time she came into contact with the thoroughly charming major. After her marriage had ended in a beastly divorce, she had vowed that never again would she form any kind of attachment toward a man. Major Monroe had a way of making her forget that promise.

In the second place, the major belonged to another woman. In these days of uncertainty, it had become common for people to snatch whatever moments of happiness were available. One never quite knew what was waiting around the corner, and it was difficult to ignore the sense of urgency that demanded she live for the day and stop worrying about tomorrow. Especially when she might never see another tomorrow.

There were certain codes that she must adhere to, however, and harboring lascivious thoughts about a married man was definitely forbidden. To do so would only bring heartache to too many people.

Nevertheless, as she climbed aboard her shiny red motorcycle, she couldn't help smiling at the thought of dining alone with the major that night. His conversations were always fascinating and amusing. Surely it couldn't hurt to enjoy his company for one evening.

Her smile faded as she chugged down the driveway. If Marlene was telling the truth that morning, and the German pilot had brutally killed a young woman, she was going to need someone to make her feel better.

CHAPTER

✂ 3 ✂

The police station was tucked behind a row of shops at the very end of the High Street. The small, white-brick building had once served as a stables when horses were the popular mode of transport. Although the renovation into headquarters for the local constabulary had taken place at least twenty years ago, Elizabeth swore she could still smell horses whenever she walked into the damp, musty room used as the front office.

The chair behind the deeply scarred desk was empty, but voices could be heard muttering behind the closed door of the back room. Whatever the conversation was about, it had to be meaningful, since no one, apparently, had heard the tinkling of the bell on the door.

Elizabeth coughed loudly. The voices continued without a break. Growing impatient, she peeled off one of her gloves and rapped on the desk with her knuckles.

The voices stopped abruptly, and a second or two later

the door opened. P.C. George Dalrymple's round, benevolent face appeared in the gap. Upon sight of his visitor, the door widened, and he hurried forward. "Lady Elizabeth! I'm so sorry, m'm. Didn't hear you come in. Have you been waiting long?"

"Not too long." Without waiting to be asked, Elizabeth plopped herself down on the visitor's chair. "I tried to ring you, but there was no answer."

George's eyes slid sideways. "Oh, yes, well, we just got back, Sid and I. Had a bit of business to take care of in town."

"That business wouldn't have anything to do with a young lady from the Macclesby farm, by any chance?"

George's gaze snapped back to her face, and he drew a hand across the shiny bald dome of his head. "Ah, well, I'm not at liberty to say, m'm."

Elizabeth crossed her ankles and folded her hands in her lap. "Now, George, you know perfectly well that you can't keep anything a secret in this village. I heard that the body of a land girl has been found in the woods. Am I correct?"

"I'd like very much to know how you found out about that, m'm, if you don't mind me asking?"

So it was true. Elizabeth's heart sank. "I found out the same way one finds out about everything going on in Sitting Marsh." She fixed a stern eye on George's worried face. "You might as well stop worrying about giving me information, George. The local grapevine is only a half step behind you."

"That may well be, m'm, but I'd be breaking the rules if I told you anything about the investigation at this point."

Elizabeth sighed. She had played this game so often. She'd have to pry the information out of him. Fortunately that wasn't as difficult as George would have her believe. "So you do admit there is an investigation going on, then?"

George lifted his face to the ceiling. "I think we can safely say that."

"And the dead body of a land girl was found in the woods?"

"I'm not denying that."

"From the Macclesby farm?"

"I believe that might be so."

"Do you know her name?"

"I believe we do."

"Can you at least give me her first name?"

George laced his fingers across his chest. "She had a hankie with her initials embroidered on it. First two letters of the alphabet."

"AB?"

He nodded.

"Do you have any suspects?"

He lowered his chin. "If I did, m'm, it might be a little difficult bringing him to justice. Since he's disappeared, if you get my meaning."

Elizabeth narrowed her eyes. "Are you talking about the German pilot who escaped yesterday?"

"Seems that way."

"What makes you think he's the killer?"

He shrugged. "Right place at the wrong time, mostly. Can't be too many dangerous criminals running around Hawthorn Woods."

"So you have no real proof."

George looked uncomfortable. "Who else would want to cut open a young girl's head with an axe? Only someone who didn't want to be taken prisoner, that's who. She was killed some time last night. The same day a German pilot lands in the village and escapes into the woods. Too much of a coincidence if you ask me."

Elizabeth thought about the young man standing shivering on the village green. "You found the axe?"

"No, m'm. Not yet. We reckon he buried it in the woods. We're asking the army blokes to help us find it. They're already looking for him, so it'll just be a matter of time—" He broke off and slapped a hand over his mouth. "You didn't hear me say any of that."

"I heard you bloody say all of that," Sid's deep voice said from the back room.

Elizabeth rose. "Don't worry, George. I won't pass any of it on. Has anyone been out to the farm to inform Sheila Macclesby?"

"Not yet, m'm. The next of kin have to be informed first. Then we have to make arrangements to recover the body."

"Well, why don't you do that, and I'll run over and let Sheila know. If she doesn't know already."

George looked doubtful, and Elizabeth forestalled any objections he might raise.

"I'm going out that way, anyway," she said firmly as she crossed the room to the door. "I'll save you the trip. I'll tell Sheila you'll be out to ask her some questions later."

"Well, I don't know as if that's a good idea—"

"I think you should get on the phone right away and ring those poor parents," Elizabeth said gently. "I'm sure they'll want to make arrangements to come down here."

George's expression changed, and Elizabeth felt a pang of sympathy. It had to be so difficult to break such beastly news. She left quickly, before George could come up with a good reason why she couldn't go out to the Macclesby farm. She very much wanted the chance to talk to Sheila before George added the woman to his official investigation. People tended to talk more freely if they thought they were simply gossiping.

On the way out there, Elizabeth did her best to curb the feeling of anticipation. A young girl had been brutally murdered, and this was no time to rejoice in the fact that she was hot on the trail of a murderer. Yet she couldn't contain the feeling of excitement at once more being involved in a murder case.

Ever since her parents had died two years earlier, she had struggled to take her father's place in the village.

Having lived in London until then, it had taken a great deal of effort to overcome the mistrust of the tenants in Sitting Marsh. She could understand their reluctance to accept her as their new administrator. The vast estate of the Manor House, which included the cottages in the village and the land upon which the High Street and its shops were built, had been overseen by earls for centuries.

This was the first time the village's main benefactor and protector had been a woman, and the daughter of a commoner, no less. Although Elizabeth had grown up at the Manor House, she had always been aware of a certain undercurrent whenever she had been in contact with the villagers. From the moment she inherited the Manor House and its holdings, she'd been determined to wipe out that aura of distrust.

She had worked hard, forming committees and making sure she was accessible to everyone who lived on the estate. She had literally gone from house to house, meeting all her tenants face-to-face, doing her best to answer all of their concerns. Her dedication had paid off, and with the exception of one or two dissidents, she now felt reasonably certain of being accepted and respected by the villagers of Sitting Marsh.

The two world wars had changed many things, including the place that nobility had once held. No one was more aware of that than Elizabeth. She used it to her advantage, establishing her rightful place in the village without the traditional barriers. Yet her ancestral home stood as a symbol of the old world, and she knew that most inhabitants of Sitting Marsh found comfort in that.

She had pledged her life to serve her people, but her struggle to maintain the Manor House, thanks to the squandering of her inheritance by her ex-husband, was painful and often thankless. Helping the constabulary to solve a murder gave her something meaningful—a sense of achievement and an excitement in her life that at times seemed so dreary without her parents.

Reaching the farmhouse, Elizabeth parked her motor-cycle outside of the main gates. No one was about in the yard as she approached the weathered porch. The land girls were already out in the fields, and no doubt Maurice, Sheila Macclesby's son, would be busy in the cowsheds.

Elizabeth lifted the lion's head door knocker and let it fall with a loud rap. It was some time before the door opened and a tousled head peered around it.

"Good morning!" Elizabeth said brightly. "I hope I'm not disturbing you."

"Oh, my." The woman clutched the neck of her faded dressing gown. "Lady Elizabeth! Whatever is the time?" She twisted her head to look back into the room. "I had no idea it was so late. Please come in, if you'll excuse the mess."

She pulled the door open wider, and Elizabeth stepped past her into a large living room dominated by a low-beamed ceiling.

"I do apologize," Sheila Macclesby said, closing the door again. "I think I'm catching a cold or something. The only time I oversleep is when I'm ill." She glanced across the room to where a large mantel clock sat above a roomy fireplace. "I wonder why Maurice didn't wake me."

"Perhaps he wanted you to rest," Elizabeth said kindly. She was being diplomatic. Maurice Macclesby had fallen from the roof of a barn when he was four years old. The accident had left him lame in one leg and damaged his brain. Maurice's mind had never pro-gressed much beyond childhood. Even so, he managed to do his fair share of the farm work, and Elizabeth admired him greatly for rising above his limitations.

"He must be wondering where I am." Sheila waved a hand at a roomy couch. "Sit down, Lady Elizabeth. Would you care for some tea?"

"Thank you, no." Now that she was here, Elizabeth

was feeling decidedly uneasy. The bad news she had
brought was bound to be a great shock to Sheila. "Have
you heard from Walter lately?"

Sheila sat down on a dining room chair with a thump.
"Wally? I got a letter from him a few days ago, from
Belgium. He's all right, isn't he?"

Annoyed with herself, Elizabeth hastened to reassure
her. "As far as I know. That's not why I'm here."

"Then, if you don't mind my asking, m'm, why *are*
you here?"

Sheila still had that drawn look on her face—and a
pallor that suggested she might be right about catching
a cold. Feeling immensely sorry for the poor woman,
Elizabeth said gently, "I'm afraid I do have bad news,
Sheila. One of your land girls was found dead in the
woods this morning."

"No!" Sheila's hand flew to her throat. "My God.
Who would do such a thing?"

"That hasn't been determined yet. P.C. Dalrymple will
be along a little later on to ask you some questions, but
I wanted to let you know what had happened to her.
You must be wondering."

"Wondering?"

"Why she didn't come home last night. The constable
believes she was killed last night."

"Oh." Sheila shook her head, as if trying to clear her
mind. "Well, I wouldn't know, would I. Since I haven't
been outside the house yet this morning, I wouldn't
know one was missing, and they often come in late at
night after I'm asleep. As a matter of fact, I heard Amelia talking to someone outside my bedroom window late
last night long after I'd gone to bed."

"Amelia?"

Sheila looked confused again. "Amelia Brunswick.
She's one of the land girls. Arguing with someone, she
was."

A. B. Elizabeth drew a deep breath. "Sheila, I'm sorry

to tell you this, but I believe it's Amelia's body they found in the woods."

Sheila stared at her for several seconds. "Oh, no, you can't mean it. Not Amelia."

"I'm afraid so."

Sheila shook her head. "She was such a bright young thing. I can't believe she's gone. The others are going to be so upset. Poor Maisie, she's such a nervous little cow. This will scare her to death."

"Maisie is one of the land girls?"

Sheila dragged a large handkerchief out of her pocket and loudly blew her nose. "We have four. Or we did until now. Pauline and Kitty are the other two. Oh, whoever done this to poor Amelia should be hung."

"He probably will be," Elizabeth said dryly. "Do you happen to know who it was Amelia was talking to last night?"

"No, m'm, I'm afraid I don't. I only heard Amelia's voice clearly. The other one was too muffled to even tell if it was a man or a woman. I just stayed in bed and pulled the covers over my ears. After all, it's none of my business what they get up to in their free time. As long as they do their work around here, I stay out of their private lives."

"Did Amelia make a habit of coming home late?"

Sheila stared down at the handkerchief and twisted it around her hands. "She liked the boys, I do know that. Always rushing around getting ready to go meet someone, she was. Most of the time I never knew what time she got home. She always got her jobs done, so I never asked."

"Did she have a special boyfriend?"

"If she did, I wouldn't know who it was."

Deciding she wouldn't learn much more from Sheila, Elizabeth asked, "Where are the other girls now?"

"Out in the fields. We're tilling them now that the harvesting's over."

"I'd like to have a word with them, if I may?"

Sheila glanced at the clock again. "Of course. They should be in for elevenses soon. Which reminds me. I should be getting on with my chores. Just look at me. A farmer's wife and still in my nightie. What must you think of me."

Elizabeth smiled. "Even farmers' wives become ill now and then. Don't let me keep you, please. I'll just wait here for the girls while you're getting dressed, if you don't mind."

Sheila rose to her feet, looking flustered. "Not at all, Lady Elizabeth. Make yourself comfortable. There's the morning newspaper there and a woman's magazine. I'll be making some coffee when the girls come in, so perhaps you'd care to join us. I could use your help when I tell them about poor Amelia."

Elizabeth turned her head as the door opened and a skinny young woman poked her head into the room. "Excuse me, Mrs. Macclesby, but have you seen my spade anywhere? I left it leaning against the wall last night, and now it's gone."

Sheila whirled around. "Maisie, how many times have I told you to put your things away when you've finished with them? That spade is back in the shed where it belongs. Why is it that the last place you girls look is where something belongs? Next time you leave something lying around outside, I'm going to charge you a shilling to get it back."

"Yes, Mrs. Macclesby. Sorry." Maisie's dark eyes shifted to Elizabeth for a moment, then she withdrew her head and disappeared.

Sheila sighed. "Half these girls they send us don't know one end of a spade from the other. Most of them don't have the stamina to work out in the fields all day, and they're always moaning and complaining about their sore muscles. Still, I suppose we should be grateful for the help now that the men are all off fighting in the trenches."

"We all have to make sacrifices these days, I'm

afraid." Elizabeth settled herself more comfortably on the couch. "I quite admire those young ladies for volunteering to work on the land. It isn't easy work, by any means."

"Maybe not," Sheila muttered as she crossed the room, "but they get well paid and well fed, and they're away from all that bombing. That's a lot to be thankful for, I'd say. Too bad they can't appreciate that." She opened the door that led to her narrow hallway. "I won't be a minute, Lady Elizabeth."

Elizabeth nodded. She needed time to think about the questions she wanted to ask the girls. She very much wanted to know the name of the person Amelia had spent time with the night before. Surely at least one of the girls should be able to tell her.

Idly she picked up the woman's magazine from the table in front of her and began leafing through it. Her glance fell on a picture of a man and woman seated at a long table. Each of them held a brimming glass of wine, and candlelight flickered between them as they stared into each other's eyes.

As she gazed at the picture with an intense fascination, the images changed. She imagined she saw herself seated at that table, staring into the eyes of Earl Monroe.

With a muttered exclamation she slapped the pages closed. She absolutely, definitely, positively could not entertain these silly notions about the major. He would be so embarrassed if he had the slightest inclination that she looked upon him in a certain favorable light.

She would be hideously mortified if he detected one hint that she was feeling anything other than businesslike toward him. The whole idea was so ludicrous she would have laughed out loud if it hadn't been for the tiny flicker of excitement deep inside her heart.

CHAPTER

❀ 4 ❀

Polly paused at the bottom of the back stairs. The door opened out onto the courtyard, and she could hear an engine revving up outside. Her heart raced to keep up with the sound. Sam could be just a few feet away from her right now. Just one quick look, that's all she wanted. It had been so long since she'd seen him, she could hardly remember what he looked like.

Obeying the irresistible urge, she dragged off her apron, undid the top two buttons of her white blouse, hitched her dark blue skirt up a couple of inches under the wide black belt she wore, then opened the door and peeked outside.

Her stomach did a double somersault when she saw the driver of the Jeep. By some miracle it was Sam, and his profile was every bit as smashing as she remembered. Her excitement propelled her forward, and before she really knew what she was doing, she'd bounced outside into the sunlight.

He saw her right away and flashed her a grin. "Well, hi, beautiful! Where have you been hiding?"

He'd called her beautiful. Entranced, Polly gazed happily at him, oblivious to the whistles and catcalls echoing across the courtyard from Sam's appreciative comrades. She wondered if it was all right to call a man beautiful, because right then, with the sun glinting on the badges on his uniform, and his teeth gleaming white in his dark, suntanned face, he was the most gorgeous thing she'd ever come close to in her life. Better than any film star she'd ever seen. Just watching him smile like that made her feel like floating all the way up to the clouds.

"What's the matter, honey? Cat got your tongue?"

She snapped out of her trance. If she wanted him to go on thinking she was a twenty-year-old woman, she'd better start behaving like one. In her best imitation of Ava Gardner, she tossed her head. "I was just wondering how long you were going to sit there making all that noise."

More whoops and whistles greeted her comment. Sam winked at her. "We're on our way out, babe. Sorry if we're disturbing you."

"Well, I do have a lot of work to do. It's hard to concentrate on the bills and everything with all this noise going on."

Sam looked around at his leering companions and climbed out of the Jeep. "Move on out. Wait for me at the end of the drive."

"Hey, Sam, no fraternizing with the natives!" one of the grinning Yanks called out as he slid into the driver's seat.

"Got any more like you at home?" another one yelled, and the rest joined in with various remarks that heated her cheeks.

"Get out of here," Sam growled at them.

As the roar of the Jeep faded away down the long, curving drive, Polly suddenly felt shy. She stared down at her serviceable black shoes and wished she'd worn the high-heeled sandals she'd splashed her coupons on last month.

"What are you doing out here?" Sam asked. "I thought you worked in the office at the other end of the house."

"I do," Polly said, crossing her fingers behind her. "I had to run an errand, that's all. I'm on my way back there now."

Sam nodded, his brown eyes intent on her face. "Haven't seen you around much."

That's because she'd spent her time avoiding all of them, Polly thought wistfully. She had to talk to Lady Elizabeth again and beg her to give her a job in the office. The last thing in the world she wanted was for Sam to find out she was only a housemaid. "What happened to Clay?" she asked, more to change the subject than anything. "He told Marlene he'd meet her at the pub, but he never turned up." It was a mild rebuke of sorts. Marlene had met Clay the same night she'd met Sam, and neither one of the men had kept their promise to meet them down the pub the next night.

Sam's gaze drifted over to the beech trees lining the drive. "Sorry about that. Clay didn't come back from a mission. I didn't feel like going into town without him."

Polly felt as if someone had slammed a fist in her stomach. "Oh, blimey, I'm so sorry. Poor Clay. Doesn't anyone know what happened to him?"

Sam shrugged. "I saw him bail out. If he's lucky he got picked up by the Resistance. If not, he'll spend the rest of the war in a POW camp."

Tears clouded her eyes, and she blinked them back. "I'll tell Marlene. She'll be so sad. She really liked him."

"Yeah. He was a nice guy."

In spite of the warmth from the sun, her insides felt like they'd been dipped in ice. It could be Sam the next

time. She couldn't bear to think of him locked up in a
prison camp. "Are you going up today?"

"Probably." He glanced at his watch. "I'd better get
going." His gaze shifted to her face again. "Wanna meet
me at the pub tonight?"

She nodded eagerly. "I'll try. About eight o'clock?"

"If I can make it."

He'd said the words casually enough, but she knew
what they meant. What he really meant was *if I come
back.*

Just then a shrill voice screeched from behind her,
"Polly? What in the world are you doing?"

"I'll see you then," Polly said hurriedly and waved
her hand before spinning around.

Violet marched toward her with a grim look on her
pinched face, Polly's discarded apron flapping in her
hand.

Polly held her breath until she heard the crunch of
Sam's footsteps gradually taper off in the distance. Violet stood waiting a few feet away, with arms crossed
and a scowl as dark as thunderclouds.

"I came out to see what all the noise was about," Polly
said, darting past the birdlike woman to the door.

"Oh? And did your apron just happen to fall off on
the way out?" The housekeeper brandished the white
cloth in her face. "And how did your skirt get all
bunched up like that? Your knees are showing. Blinking
disgraceful, that's what I call it."

"Oh, don't get your knickers in a twist." Polly tugged
at her skirt, then snatched the offending article of clothing from Violet's skinny hand. "I was just being polite,
that's all."

"Hmmph!" Violet snorted. "If you ask me, there's entirely too much of this sort of thing going on. I knew
there'd be trouble if them Yanks moved in, that I did. I
warned Lady Elizabeth, but she wouldn't listen to me,
oh, no."

Polly tugged at the strings of her apron and tied them

securely around her waist. "If you ask me, it's the nosy old biddies around here what causes all the trouble."

"Here! Mind your tongue, my girl, or I'll have you thrown out on your ear, so help me I will."

"Yeah? And who do you think will come up here and clean this house for Lady Liza then? No one, that's who. There ain't anyone in Sitting Marsh who'd do what I do, and that's a fact."

"Really." Violet stomped past her into the shadowed hallway. "Well, there are a good few women in North Horsham who would be only too glad to have a job like this. Especially when they get all that free time and their food thrown in."

"There's not enough money in it to pay their bus fare." Confident of her position, Polly picked up her bucket and turned her back on Violet. "So you'd better be nice to me, or I'll leave and go work in the factory. So there."

"Polly."

She was tempted to ignore Violet's command, but something in the older woman's tone turned her head. "What?"

"I've got something to tell you. Your sister called here this morning."

Alarmed, Polly turned all the way around. "Marlene? She's all right, isn't she? What did she call for? Is it Ma? It's not Dad, is it?" Fear made her voice crack. "Oh, Gawd, don't tell me it's Dad!"

"There's nothing wrong with any of your family as far as I know," Violet said crisply. "There is something you should know, though. One of the local land girls was found murdered in the woods this morning. Your sister called to warn you, and Lady Elizabeth wanted me to tell you she'll make some arrangements to get you a lift home this evening, so you don't have to ride your bicycle past the woods."

Polly barely heard the rest of Violet's words. She was too hung up on the news of the murder. She sat down hard on the bottom stair, trying to make sense of what she'd heard. "A land girl? Who was she? Who done it, then?"

Violet shook her head. "I don't know who she was, but it looks like that German pilot who got away yesterday killed the poor little mite. He must have been hiding in the woods, and the poor girl just happened to come across him."

Polly frowned. "What was she doing in the woods all alone, anyway? I thought those girls always went around together."

"Well, apparently this one didn't." Violet massaged the sides of her forehead with her fingers. "Anyway, get on with your work. I'm going back to the kitchen. All this upset has given me a headache."

Polly moved aside to allow her to pass her on the stairs. She couldn't believe it. Another murder in Sitting Marsh. Things had certainly changed since the Yanks had come to town. But at least they couldn't blame this on the Yanks. Polly thought about the German bomber pilot hiding in the woods and shivered. Thank goodness someone was going to take her home tonight.

She pulled herself to her feet, then her pulse leapt as an idea blazed in her head. Maybe she could get Sam to take her home. Blissfully forgetting about the murder, she began a daydream about Sam and her alone in the Jeep under the stars—a dream that would last her the entire day.

The three land girls, all of whom were strangers to Elizabeth, seemed suitably impressed when Sheila introduced her visitor as the lady of the manor. Pauline, a stocky redhead and obviously the leader of the group, startled everybody when she demanded in her strident voice, "Did you come about the murder, m'm?"

Maisie stared down at her feet, while Kitty's pudgy face turned a bright red. Elizabeth studied their reactions with interest and made a mental note to question them all individually.

"How did you hear about that?" Sheila spluttered, obviously put out at being robbed of her big announcement.

Pauline shrugged. "Biggs told me. He got it from the milkman when he came to pick up the milk this morning. He said it were a poacher what came across the body."

Sheila's face was quite pale as she stared at Pauline. "Did Biggs tell you who had been murdered?"

The girl looked uncomfortable. "No," she said slowly, "but we all think it might be Amelia, 'cause she never came back from her date last night."

"You're sure she didn't come back?" Elizabeth asked.

Pauline exchanged looks with the other girls. "Well, m'm, her bed hadn't been slept in. We all went to bed early, but Amelia slipped out to meet her boyfriend. When we woke up this morning we saw she hadn't come back."

"And you didn't say anything to Mrs. Macclesby?"

"Yes," Sheila put in, "why didn't you tell me?"

Pauline's chin shot up. "Well, you was asleep when we got up. You always told us not to disturb you in the mornings, so we made a cup of tea and a jam sandwich and then went to work. Then, when Biggs told us a land girl had been murdered, we all decided it had to be Amelia. There didn't seem much point in telling you she was missing after that."

"I hope you didn't use more than a teaspoonful of jam," Sheila said crossly. "That stuff is rationed, you know."

"Tell me what isn't," Pauline grumbled.

Maisie, who seemed to be the most disturbed by the news, looked at Elizabeth. "Excuse me, Lady Elizabeth, but did the police find out who killed Amelia?"

"We all know who did it," Sheila declared before Elizabeth could answer. "I was thinking about it while

I was upstairs. It had to be that German pilot who ran off yesterday. Who else would want to hurt such a nice young lady?"

"I can think of a few," Pauline murmured.

"Hush!" Sheila said curtly. "Do not speak ill of the dead. Go into the kitchen, all of you, and make some coffee for Lady Elizabeth and me. And bring a plate of those broken biscuits." She looked apologetically at Elizabeth. "Sorry they're in pieces, but I get them off-ration, and they taste the same as if they were whole."

"Of course," Elizabeth assured her. "But don't worry on my account. A cup of tea will be enough for me."

The girls disappeared into the kitchen and, judging from the whisperings going on, were discussing the untimely death of their unfortunate colleague. Elizabeth would have given a week's sugar ration to overhear what they were talking about.

Sheila chose that moment, however, to speculate on the whereabouts of the German pilot, and Elizabeth had to content herself with the prospect of questioning the girls later.

After sampling some of the mushy, stale pieces of broken biscuits, she swallowed down her tea too fast to be genteel, then quickly made her excuses to Sheila, who seemed unflatteringly relieved to let her go.

Thick white clouds scudded across the sky, promising a squall from the ocean as Elizabeth picked her way across the fields to where Kitty sat perched on a wagon. The land girl's attempts to urge the weary-looking horse to pull her alongside the sheaves of corn were met with stubborn resistance. The other two girls waited impatiently, ready to toss the corn into the cart with long, unwieldy pitchforks.

In spite of Maisie's frail appearance, she seemed to have no trouble lifting a sheaf of corn with the clumsy implement. Elizabeth was quite sure she herself could never have managed it, nor did she have any desire to attempt it. She tapped Maisie on the shoulder and noticed that the girl started quite violently as she dropped the pitchfork.

"Sorry, your ladyship," she muttered. "I didn't see you coming."

"I didn't mean to startle you," Elizabeth said, giving her an encouraging smile. "I was just wondering if I could have a quick word with you."

"If you're going to ask her about Amelia," Pauline said shortly, "she doesn't know anything we don't know."

"I'm sure she doesn't," Elizabeth glanced at Pauline's sullen face, "but I didn't want to interrupt all of you at once."

The horse, apparently tired of all the screeching and jerking of his reins, took a few reluctant steps forward. Pauline heaved her sheaf into the wagon, and Elizabeth seized the opportunity to draw Maisie aside.

"I just wanted to ask you how well you knew Amelia," she said, ignoring Pauline's baleful glances in their direction.

Maisie seemed as if she wanted to run away and hide. "Not very well," she said, her voice trembling on a sob. "She wasn't as friendly as the rest of us. I don't like to speak ill of the dead, m'm, but Amelia didn't really belong with us, if you know what I mean. She was always bragging about her big fancy house and cars, and how she went horse-riding and had ballet lessons and everything."

"I see." Elizabeth glanced over at Pauline, but she had moved on to the next sheaf and was out of earshot. "What about the rest of the girls? How did they feel about Amelia?"

Maisie's gaze flicked to Pauline for a second. "They didn't like her neither. Especially Pauline. Amelia stole her boyfriend from the army camp. Pauline had it in for her after that."

Elizabeth narrowed her eyes.

As if reading her thoughts, Maisie added hurriedly,

"She wouldn't have killed her, though, m'm. Honest. I mean, she couldn't have, could she. Pauline went to bed the same time as the rest of us. We sleep in the same room, and our floor creaks something terrible. I would have heard if she'd got out of bed."

Elizabeth patted the frightened girl's shoulder. "It's all right, Maisie. I'm not accusing anyone. Do you know who Amelia was meeting last night?"

Maisie clutched the pitchfork to her chest as if for support. "It was probably Pauline's old boyfriend, Jeff Thomas, m'm. He's a lieutenant out at the army camp in Beerstowe." She pinched her lips together, as if afraid of what she'd said.

"Don't worry," Elizabeth said, feeling sorry for the girl. "You're not doing anything wrong. I appreciate you telling me all this. It could be extremely helpful in finding out who murdered that poor girl." She paused, watching an array of conflicting emotions chase across Maisie's thin face. "Is there anything else you want to tell me?"

Maisie swallowed a few times, then said in a rush, "I don't want to get no one in trouble, Lady Elizabeth, but I don't want you to go blaming Jeff, neither. He's a nice lad, that Jeff, and he wouldn't hurt no one. If you ask me, it's Maurice you should be talking to, that's who."

Elizabeth raised her eyebrows. "Maurice? What makes you say that?"

Maisie sent a hunted look in the direction of the farmhouse. "He was always hanging around Amelia. Fancied her, he did. Amelia wouldn't have none of it, though. Told him to shove off. She told us she was afraid of him, and Amelia was never afraid of no one except him."

Feeling greatly disturbed, Elizabeth thanked the girl and watched her hurry off to join the others. Try as she might, she could not picture Maurice Macclesby in the role of murderer. True, he could be somewhat unsettling to be around. With his pronounced limp and vacant stare, not to mention the scruffy chin thanks to his inept and apparently infrequent efforts to shave, he was not a comfortable person to be around. Still, she would never have considered him violent.

She tackled Pauline next who, unlike Maisie, was obviously bursting to tell her what she knew. "That Amelia was nothing but a greedy, two-faced snob," she announced, stabbing the ground with her pitchfork for emphasis. "I always said something bad would happen to her one day. Though I never thought she'd be done in. Especially by someone like Maurice."

Startled, Elizabeth fastened her gaze on the young woman's face. "Does everyone think Maurice killed Amelia?"

Pauline shrugged. "I don't know about everyone else. The milkman reckons it was that German pilot. All I know is that Maurice was really soppy about Amelia, and she couldn't stand him near her. She told him that more than once, but he never took no notice. Kept following her around, staring at her in that funny way of his like she was a film star or something. Mind you, she was really pretty, I suppose, in a prissy kind of way. All that blond hair and blue eyes. She didn't half fancy herself, I tell you."

Elizabeth closely watched Pauline's expression when she said quietly, "I understand you were a friend of Amelia's boyfriend, Lieutenant Jeff Thomas?"

Pauline flinched visibly. "I was. Not anymore. Good riddance to him, that's what I say. If he wants to be taken in by all that talk, then he's not worth caring about."

"Amelia had gone out to meet him last night, I understand."

"I don't know who she went out with. The rest of us went to bed. I have to get my sleep to do this kind of work."

"And you didn't hear her come back?"

Pauline shook her head. "She never came back. Her bed wasn't slept in."

"You didn't hear anyone talking outside the house late last night?"

"Never heard a thing." Pauline sent her a sly look. "Why? Did someone see her come back? Was it Maurice? I knew it. I bet he waited for her in the dark then went for her. Wonder what her father will say to all this."

Maurice again. Elizabeth frowned. "Do you know Amelia's father?"

"No, 'course not. He's some big fancy attorney in London. Got pots of money. That's if Amelia was telling the truth. Though I wouldn't put it past her to make it all up. Never did like her. She was too full of herself, that girl."

"Well, thank you for your help." Elizabeth had noticed Kitty climbing down from the wagon and wanted to speak to the girl before she disappeared.

"Kitty doesn't know anything, neither," Pauline said, following Elizabeth's gaze. "We all went to sleep at the same time last night and woke up this morning, and none of us heard anything nor saw anything."

"Nevertheless," Elizabeth said quietly, "I'd like to have a word with her."

In that respect at least, Pauline was right. Kitty had nothing to add to the information Elizabeth had already been given. Kitty was as uncomplimentary about the murdered girl as her companions and just as certain that Maurice had been responsible.

Having satisfied herself that she would learn no more from them, Elizabeth trudged back to the farmhouse. She was now faced with the unpleasant task of questioning Maurice and she wasn't looking forward to it.

Much against her principles, she couldn't help hoping that it was the German pilot, after all, who had brutally attacked the young girl and left her broken body in the woods. He at least had some excuse. Something told her, however, that there was much more to this murder than a simple case of someone desperate to evade capture. Much as she hated to admit it, her instincts pointed in the direction of Sheila's unfortunate son. If he was indeed the killer, it would very likely break Sheila's heart.

CHAPTER

✿ 5 ✿

"Madam will be entertaining a guest in the dining room for dinner tonight," Violet told Martin, in the vague hope that he would contribute something useful to the occasion.

Martin looked up from his seat at the kitchen table. "Not before time. We haven't had any guests in the dining room for years."

"Not since the master and his wife have been gone." Violet took down a crystal glass from the cupboard above the gas stove. "It will be nice to use the good china again."

"It will be most satisfying to see madam seated in her rightful position at the dining room table." Martin reached for the newspaper and folded it neatly. "I do not feel comfortable when she sits with us here in the kitchen. Her father would be most displeased."

Violet finished polishing the glass before answering

him. "I'm afraid he'd be displeased about a good many things. Thank Gawd he's in his grave and can't see what's going on in this house."

"Ah, but that's just it." Martin began rising to his feet. It was a long and tedious process, irritating to watch. Violet turned her back on him, but even so, she had seen the performance so many times she could picture it in her mind.

Slap. That was Martin's hands hitting the table, palms down. The chair creaked when its feet scraped across the floor. It creaked again when his backside rose a few inches then plopped back on the seat.

Violet waited, counting the three groans that accompanied his attempts to push himself upright. Finally, when she heard the air rush out of his lungs in a heavy sigh, she knew he was on his feet and resting heavily on his hands. One more groan and he would be mobile again.

"That's just what?" she demanded, wondering why she bothered. Martin's comments were at best meaningless, and at worst maddeningly mysterious.

"I beg your pardon?"

Violet turned to find him peering at her over the top of his glasses. Both she and Lizzie had long ago given up explaining to the silly old fool that he'd see a lot better if he'd just look through the lenses instead of over them. As it was, for all the good they did him perched on the end of his nose like that, he might just as well put them on a cow. "You said 'that's just it.' "

"I did?" Martin's white eyebrows met over the bridge of his specs. "What was I talking about?"

"How the blazes should I know?" Violet flapped her cloth at him. "I never know what you're talking about, do I. You're always muttering about something or other that doesn't make any sense."

Martin drew himself up as straight as his bowed shoulders would allow. "I might not make any sense to you, Violet, but I make perfect sense to myself."

He was probably right at that, Violet thought grimly. "Well, we have to get the dining room table set for dinner. See if you can find Polly and tell her I'll need her help tonight. She can stay late for a change. With all this talk of murder, I forgot to tell her about it when I saw her."

As soon as the words were out of her mouth, she regretted them. Her concern was well founded.

Martin clutched his chest in the region of his heart and staggered. "Murder? Where? Here? No! When? Who? Who? *Who*?"

"For Gawd's sake, Martin, stop hooting like a bloody owl. It wasn't anyone we know, so you can just forget about it."

"Forget about it?" Martin ran a hand over his sparse wisps of hair. "Forget we have a murderer running around? We could all be slaughtered in our beds. Where is madam? It's not safe for her to be running around on her own like this. In my day young women were chaperoned everywhere."

"In my day, too." Deciding that he'd survived the shock, she took down another glass from the cupboard. "But things change, Martin, and we have to change with them."

"Not me," Martin declared stoutly. "I'm too old to change."

"If you ask me, you're too bloody old to breathe," Violet said crisply. "But that doesn't stop you trying. Now get on with you and see if you can find Polly."

"Very well, but it wouldn't hurt you to say please once in a while."

"Please." She watched him shuffle toward the door an inch at a time.

He was almost there when he paused and slowly edged his body around to face her again. "Was it one of those blasted Americans?"

She blinked. "What?"

"The person who was prematurely deprived of his life."

Irritated by his annoying habit of talking like a dictionary, Violet's voice rose a notch. "No, it wasn't. So stop worrying about it."

"Violet, I shall worry about it if I so wish. I demand to know who is the unfortunate victim of this abominable crime."

Giving up, Violet shrugged. "It was one of them land girls, that's who. Someone found her body in the woods. Mind you, the way some of them run around flaunting themselves, it's no wonder one of them came to a bad end."

"Oh, my, oh, my." Martin shook his head so hard his specs slid off. More by luck than judgement, he caught them before they fell to the floor and stuck them back on his nose. "Well, at least it didn't happen here at the manor. I did wonder if perhaps the master had a hand in it."

"A hand in what?"

"The murder." Martin swayed forward on his feet and touched his lips with a withered finger. "He doesn't like them, you know."

Violet crossed her arms and tipped her head to one side. "The master's dead, Martin. Killed by a bomb in London. Blown to bloomin' bits, you might say. They buried what was left of him in the churchyard. You were there. Even if he had risen from the dead, he'd be walking around without a head, so you wouldn't be able to bloody recognize him if you saw him."

Martin turned pale. "I say! Steady on, Violet. That's a ghastly thing to say about the master. He hasn't lost his head at all. I saw him this morning, walking along the great hall, and his head was right where it should be."

"Well, it's too bad yours isn't," Violet snapped, having reached the end of her patience. "Now, are you going to stop all this silly blabbering about ghosts and find Polly for me, or do I have to find her myself?"

Martin sniffed. "There's no need to take that tone of voice with me. I'm quite capable of finding the wretched girl. Though what good it will do I can't imagine. She spends more time gazing at herself in mirrors than taking care of her duties."

And that, Violet thought as she watched Martin shuffle out the door, was the most intelligent thing he'd said that morning.

Elizabeth crossed the barnyard and headed for the stables. Since Maurice wasn't in the fields, he was probably mucking out the stalls. There was no sign of him there, however, and she wondered if he'd gone back to the house for an early dinner. She was on her way back there when she spotted him over in the paddock, sitting on the top fence with his back to her.

The long grass muffled her footsteps as she approached. Not wanting to startle him, she called him by name, but he gave no sign of having heard her. Even when she reached his side and gently touched his arm, he remained as still as a rock.

After a moment she opened the gate and walked inside the large fenced area, where several carthorses grazed while they waited for their turn in the fields. Ignoring them, she paused in front of Maurice. He sat staring in the direction of the woods, his gaunt features calm with his usual blank expression.

"Maurice?" Elizabeth waved a hand in front of him. "I'd like to talk to you. I want you to tell me about Amelia." She watched him closely, but not a flicker of emotion touched his pallid face. His hands, however, clenched in tight fists, and she knew that he'd been told the sad news.

She tried again. "I know Amelia was a special friend. I'm so very sorry. It must hurt a lot."

The passive mask remained unbroken.

"Maurice, I know you don't want to talk about it. But

people are gossiping, and we have to find out the truth, or innocent people could get hurt very badly. You might be able to help me if you can tell me what you know."

She stared into his empty eyes, searching for a sign that he understood. She'd seen him so often talking to the horses, cows, and pigs, whispering in their ears, gentling them with his large, clumsy hands. Once she had found him crouched over a wounded bird, tears coursing down his face as he tried to pick up the poor thing. Nothing in the world could convince her that this gentle, caring person could attack an innocent young woman and hack open her head. He just wasn't capable of such violence.

"I'll find out who did it, Maurice," she said quietly. "I'll find him and I promise you I'll see he's punished."

She turned to go, but not before she'd seen a single tear squeeze out of the boy's eye and roll slowly, unheeded, down his cheek. Disturbed by the image, she made her way back to the house.

Sheila greeted her at the door, her face flushed and agitated. "Did you find out anything?" she demanded before Elizabeth could speak. "I saw you talking to Maurice. What did he say? He's upset by all this. He liked Amelia. He doesn't understand what happened."

"I believe he understands more than you think," Elizabeth said quietly. "I just wanted to warn you that P.C. Dalrymple might want to question Maurice. I think you should prepare him for that."

Apprehension burned in Sheila's eyes. "I'll do the best I can. I can't believe the police would go bothering my son. He doesn't know anything about it."

"They have to follow procedures," Elizabeth said, echoing George Dalrymple's favorite comment.

"Everyone knows that Nazi pilot killed poor Amelia. If George had an ounce of sense in that thick noggin of his, he'd be out looking for him in the woods, instead of upsetting everyone out here. What did the girls tell you, anyhow? Nothing, I bet. Nobody knows anything."

Sheila appeared to make a great effort to calm her angry torrent of words. "Begging your pardon, m'm, but it makes me cross when the police don't do their job right."

"Well, I'm sure they'll do their best," Elizabeth said cheerfully.

A shout from across the yard turned her head. Maisie stood a few yards away, waving a spade in the air. "I found it, Mrs. Macclesby. All nice and clean. Thank you!"

Sheila stared at Maisie as the girl tramped across the yard, carrying the spade over her shoulder. "I never know what these modern girls are going on about half the time," she muttered.

"Well," Elizabeth said, "I'll be leaving you alone now to get on with your work."

"Thank you, Lady Elizabeth." For the first time that day Sheila Macclesby managed a weak smile. "I appreciate you bringing the sad news to me."

"And I appreciate you allowing me to talk to the land girls." Elizabeth turned away, then paused. "You were right, of course. They knew nothing."

"I knew they didn't, m'm. It's like I said. It was that Nazi pilot. Everyone knows that."

Not everyone, Elizabeth thought as she made her way back to her motorcycle. The land girls were all convinced Maurice had killed Amelia. Not one of them had seemed particularly sad about it. In fact, so far Maurice was the only one who had shed a genuine tear over the young woman's death.

Elizabeth climbed aboard her motorcycle and bounced on the kick start. The engine fired, and she rumbled out of the farmyard and onto the road, turning over in her mind what she had learned that day.

Much as the land girls disliked the deceased woman, she didn't think any of them were responsible for her murder. Pauline seemed to have the sole motive, but according to the other two girls, she hadn't left her bed that night. That left Maurice and the German pilot with a motive for murder. There was one other person, however, who could have been responsible for Amelia's death—Lieutenant Jeff Thomas.

Right then, he seemed the most likely candidate, since she found it so hard to believe that the other two were capable of such a violent crime. Then again, it was all too easy to jump to conclusions.

Maybe she was too ready to believe the best of people. That had certainly been her downfall in her disastrous marriage. What she was certain of was that this detective business was a lot more complicated than she'd realized. No wonder George and Sid had so much trouble with it.

Speaking of whom, she reminded herself, she needed to talk to the constables and ask them to talk to Jeff Thomas. He was apparently the last person to see Amelia alive. Since it appeared he had been quarreling with her that night, he was most certainly at the top of the list of suspects. Unfortunately her connections did not stretch to His Majesty's service, and she could hardly go waltzing into an army camp demanding to speak to one of their soldiers. She'd have to leave that to the constables and hope they did their job.

In the meantime, there was the little matter of dinner with Major Monroe to deal with, and it would take her an entire afternoon to find a suitable dress to wear in her eclectic wardrobe.

Her spirits rising, Elizabeth sailed grandly down the High Street of Sitting Marsh on the saddle, acknowledging the friendly waves of the villagers with her usual graceful salute, carefully copied from the matriarch of the royal family. Image was everything, after all.

Martin took forever to open the door to her urgent summons when she reached home. By the time he'd finally dragged the door open wide enough for her to pass through, she was seething with impatience.

His look of alarm when he saw her alerted her to the fact that something had upset him—an event that seemed to be occurring with alarming frequency these days.

"Thank heaven you are home, madam," he spluttered. "I was beginning to fear for your very life. Violet tells me there is a filthy scoundrel loose in the woods. Murdered a field girl . . . or farm girl . . . or something."

Violet, Elizabeth thought darkly, *talked too much*. "It's all right, Martin. As you can see, I'm perfectly all right. But thank you for worrying about me."

"I shall always worry about you, madam. No matter what Violet tells me to do. Or not to do."

Wondering what that was about, Elizabeth left him muttering to himself and headed down to the kitchen, from where an appetizing fragrance wafted up the stairs.

Violet stood at the stove, busily stirring something in a pot. She twisted her head around when Elizabeth walked in. "Oh, there you are, Lizzie. I was wondering when you'd get back. Martin has been driving me batty with his dithering. Kept telling me you'd been murdered."

"I wish you hadn't told him," Elizabeth said mildly. "You know how easily he's upset."

Violet sniffed. "Better he heard it from me than from someone else. He's going quite dotty lately. He's convinced that the master's ghost is roaming the halls. Hope he doesn't tell the Yanks that."

"I don't think they'll pay much attention to him." Elizabeth glanced at the clock. "What are you cooking?"

"Tomato soup. Got a new loaf of crusty bread from Bessie's Bake Shop to go with it."

"Wonderful!" Elizabeth sank onto a chair at the table. "I'm absolutely starving. How is Bessie? Is she still doing a good business in the tearoom? I haven't been down there in weeks."

"She's doing better now that the Yanks are here." Violet stirred the soup one more time, then turned off the

gas flame beneath it. "The shop was full of them.
Though mind you, I think they help her out with sugar
and flour from the base. She even had two dozen eggs
in the pantry. Bet they didn't come from Bodkins."

"I'm sure she has special rations for her business,"
Elizabeth said, determined not to be drawn into another
argument about accepting gifts from the Americans.

Violet poured the steaming soup into two bowls and
set one of them in front of Elizabeth. "So what happened
down at the police station? Have they caught that bloody
German yet? I saw Rita down at the bakery. She's getting her troops together to go and hunt for him."

Alarmed, Elizabeth paused with her spoon halfway to
her mouth. "I certainly hope she does no such thing.
Does she have any idea how dangerous that can be?"

"I would think if she knows that Nazi killed someone
she'd also have the sense to know he isn't going to play
Ring around the Rosie with them."

"I was thinking more of it being dangerous for the
German."

Violet grinned. "You might have something there.
You know there's no stopping Rita once she's got a bee
in her bonnet about something. She's all set to go after
that poor blighter. Heaven help him if she catches up
with him."

"It's unlikely she will. I understand from George that
soldiers from the army camp are hunting for him. I just
hope that they don't run into Rita and her motley crew
of housewives."

"I wouldn't like to bet on who comes out best of that
battle."

Elizabeth sipped at her soup, then lowered her spoon.
"This is very good, Violet."

The housekeeper tipped her head to one side. "You
haven't told me how you got on at the police station."

Having failed in her attempt to change the subject,
Elizabeth laid down her spoon. "I don't think the constables have any real proof that the German pilot was

responsible for the murder. They say she was killed with an axe, but they haven't found it yet, so they don't really know any more than I do."

"Those nitwits never know what they're doing, anyway. That's what you get when you drag two blokes out of retirement like that. They forget everything they ever learned, and their feeble minds can't learn it again."

"They are doing the best they can under the circumstances. While I acknowledge that the German must be caught and put under guard, I have the feeling that the constables are looking in the wrong place for their murderer."

"You mean he's not in the woods?"

"I mean I don't think he's necessarily the murderer."

"Go on!" Violet brought her soup to the table and sat down. "Well, if you don't think the German killed that poor girl, then who did? Maybe it was one of the Yanks this time."

Elizabeth jerked up her chin. "I don't want to hear you repeat that to anyone else," she said sharply. "Rumors are flying around as it is, and I won't have the Americans blamed for everything that goes wrong in Sitting Marsh."

Violet looked unabashed by her attack. "All right, Lizzie, keep your hair on. I was just thinking aloud."

"I'd rather you kept that kind of thought to yourself."

Violet leaned forward and peered into her face. "Getting nervous about our dinner tonight, are we?"

"No, of course not." Elizabeth broke off a piece of bread and dropped it into her soup. "I've told you, this is a business dinner. And if you try to make anything else of it, Violet, I shall be unforgivably rude."

"Seems to me," Violet said quietly, "that you're already making a lot out of it. Just be careful, Lizzie. A lot of hearts get broken during wartime. It happens all the time."

Elizabeth chose not to answer. The warning went deep, however, and she could not ignore its message. No matter how much she tried.

CHAPTER

❧ 6 ❧

By that evening Elizabeth's stomach was so full of butterflies she was quite certain she'd never be able to force down a bite of food. Which would be a great shame, since the aromas wafting from the warm kitchen were enough to make a statue's mouth water.

Making sure she was at least ten minutes late, Elizabeth finally left the sanctuary of her bedroom and proceeded down the main staircase to the dining room.

Martin hovered at the foot of the staircase, in his usual state of flustered anxiety. "Madam," he whispered hoarsely as soon as she came within earshot, "there's one of those confounded Americans sitting in the dining room. The master is not going to like this at all. Not at all, madam. The blighter had the nerve to tell me he was invited. What utter rot! Just say the word, and I will remove him at once."

Elizabeth hid a smile at the thought of Martin attempting to forcefully remove the rugged major. "It's quite all right, Martin. I invited the major to dinner myself. Didn't Violet tell you?"

Martin looked aghast. "Violet merely mentioned that you were expecting a guest. She failed to mention that you were entertaining an *American*."

He'd said "American" as if he were referring to some obnoxious beetle. Elizabeth raised her eyebrows. "The major is a guest in our home, Martin. I trust you will treat him as such?"

Instantly transformed by her tone, Martin stiffened. "As you wish, madam. I feel obligated to point out, however, that the master has not given his permission for such an escapade, and I am quite sure that he will be as appalled as I am when he is made aware of it. We are only trying to protect you, madam."

Elizabeth patted Martin's arm. "Thank you, Martin. I appreciate your concern. And in case you might have forgotten, the master is no longer with us. He and my mother have been gone for two years."

Martin nodded. "Gone and returned, madam. As you no doubt will discover for yourself before too long."

Elizabeth frowned. Martin often had lapses of memory and frequent bouts of mind-wandering, but they rarely lasted more than a few minutes or so. His continued insistence on seeing her father's ghost was disturbing. It was something she would have to worry about later, she decided. Right now she had something much more tangible to worry about.

She had selected a calf-length cream frock in raw silk to wear and had draped a sky-blue scarf around her shoulders to soften the neckline. She really didn't care for the shoulder pads, which tended to make her look top-heavy, but it seemed that all the clothes came with them these days. Her mother's gold and pearl earrings and matching pendant completed the attire, and she felt confident she looked her best.

Even so, she felt like a gawky schoolgirl when Martin

pompously announced her arrival in the dining room with just an underlying hint of disapproval.

Major Earl Monroe was seated at the foot of the table. He rose to his feet as she walked into the elegant room, and she found his unabashed expression of appreciation even more unsettling.

She murmured her apologies while he pulled back her chair. "I'm terribly sorry for keeping you waiting, Major."

He eased the chair in as she sat down, then returned the length of the table to his own seat. "No need to apologize, Lady Elizabeth. I've been enjoying an excellent Scotch while I studied the contents of this room. You have some great antiques on these walls. Fascinating stuff."

She smiled. "Thank you. Some of them have been in the family for generations."

"Like the portraits upstairs. What about that whalebone over there? What's the story behind that?"

Thankful to have an opening subject to break the ice, she launched into the story of her great-great-uncle's adventures aboard a sailboat in the Pacific islands.

Violet interrupted a few minutes later to announce the menu; celery soup, roast beef, and Yorkshire pudding, followed by a sherry trifle. "I'll be serving the first course in a moment or two," she declared. "Meanwhile, can I offer you a glass of champagne?"

Elizabeth widened her eyes in surprise. "That would be very nice, Violet." Wondering how on earth her housekeeper had acquired champagne, she added, "You remember Major Monroe, Violet? I'm sure you remember my housekeeper, Major?"

"We bumped into each other in the kitchen just now." He exchanged a look with Violet that was purely conspiratorial, and she preened like a mating peacock.

"The major was kind enough to bring us a bottle or two. That's where the champagne came from." A flush spread over her cheeks, and she patted her frizzy hair. "He brought whiskey as well."

Put out by the housekeeper's defiance of her wishes, Elizabeth said tartly, "You may serve the champagne, Violet."

Violet's expression was unrepentant. "I'll send Martin in," she said and scuttled back to the kitchen.

"I hope I didn't break any of your customs by taking the bottles to the kitchen."

Elizabeth stared down the table at him. Separated by three ornate silver candelabra, two huge bowls of white daisies, and a cornucopia filled with ripe apples from the orchard, she felt less intimidated by him than during their earlier encounters. Even so, she felt the impact of his gaze as she murmured, "Not at all, Major. I'm sure Violet was most appreciative."

He chuckled. "She gave me a hug. Nice lady. Reminds me of an aunt of mine back home."

Elizabeth felt a pang of envy and quickly suppressed it. She had no desire to hug the major. If Violet wanted to make a fool of herself that was her affair. "Violet has been with the family a very long time. I value her as a friend and as a surrogate member of my family. She was a great source of comfort to me after the death of my parents."

Violet chose that moment to return with the champagne. She fluttered around Earl as if he were a long-lost son, Elizabeth noticed, with a faint pang of resentment. It was obvious the major had won over Violet with his undeniable charm. All the more reason for her to remain on guard as far as her own attitude toward the handsome American. It wouldn't do for everyone to fall under his spell.

She was beginning to understand now the attraction these men held in the village. Much more debonair and infinitely more glamourous than their British stiff-upper-lip counterparts, they added the spice of adventure to a very bleak environment for the women of Sitting Marsh.

Forced to manage without their menfolk, struggling to feed and clothe their families on the meager rations allowed them, faced with uncertain futures at best, no wonder they welcomed such exciting and alluring newcomers with open arms.

They would all do well to heed Violet's warnings. She had spoken the truth when she'd said that many hearts were broken in wartime. The understandable urge to live for the moment was a powerful aphrodisiac. Under such circumstances, even the most level-headed person could well stray from the straight and narrow path.

"Why the glum look? You don't like the champagne?"

Startled out of her thoughts, she quickly lifted her glass. Bubbles danced before her eyes as she murmured, "To your good health, Major Monroe."

Instead of answering her, he rose from his chair. "Can I ask a favor?"

Wary now, she put down the glass. "Of course."

"Do I have to sit at the end of this table? I feel like I'm trying to talk to you from the opposite end of a jungle."

She hesitated, torn between fear of losing her security and the very strong desire to have him sit closer. In the end, desire won. She waved a hand at the chair to her right. "Please, make yourself at home."

He grinned, unsettling her even further as he sat down in the chair she'd indicated. "That's better. Now I can hear you and see you. I was beginning to get lonely down there."

Matching his light tone, she murmured, "Well, we can't have that, can we. I wouldn't want it spread about that the Hartleighs were inhospitable."

"I thought there was only one Hartleigh now."

She smiled. "Only one in residence. I have uncles, aunts, and various cousins scattered around the world. Most of them live abroad."

"What happened to your parents?"

His abrupt question disturbed her. She took a moment to regroup her thoughts.

"I'm sorry . . . if you'd rather not answer—"

"No, it's all right." She took a sip of her champagne and was pleasantly surprised by the delicate flavor. "This is very good."

"I'm glad you like it."

She liked the way his eyes crinkled at the corners when he smiled. His skin looked leathery, dried out from too much sun and wind. She felt an instant's longing to see the land where he'd grown up then quickly began speaking in an effort to erase the treacherous thought. "My parents were in London attending a concert two years ago, during the Blitz. My mother didn't want to go, but my father insisted. He was not about to let those filthy Nazis, as he called them, stop him from living his life. They were waiting for a taxi when the sirens sounded. On their way to the shelter a bomb landed just down the street. They were both killed instantly."

She sat staring down at her glass while the silence seemed to stretch into hours.

Then Earl Monroe gently covered her hand with his. "I'm sorry. That must have been real tough."

She gulped. "It was."

The door swung open and crashed against the wall, startling them both. Earl snatched his hand away, while Elizabeth sat up straight, trying to look as if nothing out of the ordinary had just happened.

Martin shuffled into the room, bearing a tray upon which a large soup tureen balanced at a somewhat precarious angle. "Soup, madam!" he shouted, making her jump.

"Thank you, Martin." Elizabeth eyed the priceless tureen, wondering what on earth had possessed Violet to entrust it to his unsteady hands. "You may put it down here."

Quickly she cleared a space for it near her plate, then watched in trepidation as Martin advanced one uncertain step at a time, bearing his burden as if it were a sacrifice being offered to the gods.

Holding her breath, she waited for him to reach the table, ready to spring into action should his step falter. When it happened, she was unprepared for it after all.

Martin tilted the tray just a fraction, but it was enough to start the heavy tureen sliding toward the edge. Elizabeth froze, certain that her butler would be badly scalded by the hot soup. Before she had time to let out her breath, however, Earl had leapt from his chair and somehow rounded the table in time to grab the tureen by its handles.

"We'll just put it down here, sir," he said and deposited the precious china pot safely onto the white linen tablecloth without spilling a drop.

Martin's eyebrows twitched a few times. "I say, sir. Magnificent catch. Couldn't have done better myself. Make a good silly mid-on proud, that one would."

Catching sight of Earl's puzzled look, Elizabeth murmured, "Cricket term." She turned to Martin, who was still gazing at the major with something like awe on his face. "You may leave the soup, Martin. I will serve it myself." She waited for Earl to reseat himself, still with a bemused expression on his face.

He sat down heavily on his chair as Martin shuffled slowly out of the room. "Silly mid-on?"

"Yes, it's a cricket fielder's position."

"Silly mid-on? For real?"

Elizabeth nodded. "They have a silly mid-off, too."

"You're kidding me."

"I swear I'm not." She didn't think this was a good time to explain all the intricacies of one of England's favorite pastimes. "Would you care for some soup?"

He obediently held out his plate. "This is one game I've got to see."

"Well, I'm afraid you might have a long wait." She carefully ladled pale green soup into the deep bowl. "The men who usually play cricket on the green have all been called up. I suppose the army might have a game now and then, though I imagine if they do it would be played at the camp."

"That's too bad." Earl put his plate down in front of him and eyed it suspiciously. "I'd like to have seen a cricket match."

"Well, maybe we can arrange something one of these days." She watched him take a cautious sip of the soup and was pleased when his expression cleared. "I trust the soup is to your liking?"

He flashed a grin at her. "The soup is very much to my liking. Thanks."

She quickly transferred her attention to her own dish.

"You must have been lonely growing up in this huge house," he said, after a few moments of companionable silence.

She laid down her spoon and dabbed at her mouth with her serviette. "Not really. We had more servants then, and the house was always full of guests. My mother entertained a lot. Though I often wished I could have gone to school instead of having a private tutor. I think I missed a lot."

He studied her with a grave expression. "I guess you did. What about now? This can't be much of a life for a woman like yourself, living practically alone in a mansion."

"Oh, I have plenty of companionship. Violet, Martin, and Polly are like family, and I have my various committees, and there are always people coming in from the village for advice or help with a problem. Though I must admit, I have been thinking lately of adopting a couple of dogs for extra companionship. There was always a dog around when I was growing up."

The major smiled. "Didn't you ever want to break free of all this and go see the rest of the world?"

She laughed, not quite hiding the bitterness. "Oh, I did all that. I traveled fairly extensively and lived in London for several years until I divorced my husband."

He sounded surprised when he said, "Oh, I'm sorry. I didn't realize you were married."

"Almost nine years. Harry is a compulsive gambler. When my parents died I inherited everything. We moved down here to take over the management of the estate, and Harry managed to lose most of my inheritance in a little over a year. I divorced him before he could lose the Manor House as well."

"Sounds like you were well rid of him."

"Maybe, but it's such a dreadful stigma to be divorced. Especially when one is the lady of the manor. I lost the respect of the villagers. It didn't help that their new guardian is a woman. If it hadn't been for the fact that it's wartime and most of the able-bodied men are serving abroad, I would have had a much harder time of it."

"Surely in this day and age people are more understanding about divorce. It happens all the time now."

"In your country, perhaps. Possibly even here, in the large cities. But in a small village like Sitting Marsh, divorce is still frowned upon. It has taken me many months to earn back the respect of the villagers. Even now, there are one or two who look upon me with disdain."

"Surely not. You are every inch a lady, and I drink to that." He raised his glass with a flourish, warming the chill in her heart.

"Thank you. I appreciate the kind words, spoken by a true gentleman." She tapped the rim of his glass with her own.

She was still staring into his eyes when the door swung open, and Polly rushed in.

The housemaid stopped short at the sight of madam and the American gazing at each other across the candlelit table. "Sorry," she muttered. "Am I interrupting something?"

Feeling as if she'd been caught cheating at cards, Elizabeth cleared her throat. "What are you doing here, Polly? Why haven't you gone home?"

Polly shrugged, then stacked the empty soup bowls into the tureen with a loud clatter that made Elizabeth wince. "Violet asked me to stay and help out with the dinner, m'm. I was wondering if you'd arranged for my lift home tonight? Violet said you didn't want me riding my bicycle." She sent a sly look at Earl, who looked at Elizabeth for clarification.

"Oh, yes, of course." Elizabeth gave Earl an apologetic smile. "I wonder if perhaps one of your men could take Polly home? I hate to ask, but with a suspected murderer running around loose in the woods, I really don't think it's safe for her to ride home alone on her bicycle."

She saw the shock in his eyes and was immediately contrite. "Oh, I'm so sorry, Major. I assumed you'd heard—"

He shook his head. "I've heard nothing. I've been gone all day, and after I checked in at the base I came straight back here."

"It was a land girl," Polly told him with relish. "They reckon that German what escaped yesterday killed her. Found her body this morning in the woods with her head chopped off."

"That's enough, Polly," Elizabeth said sharply. "You may take the plates out now."

"Yes, m'm." Polly picked up the loaded tureen. "But what about my ride?"

"I'll arrange something," Earl said. "What time do you want to leave?"

"After you finish your meal will be fine, sir. Thank you." Polly paused at the door, cradling the heavy dish in her arms. "It would be nice if Sam Cutter could take me home, sir. I'd really like that."

Elizabeth raised her eyebrows, while Earl looked speculative. "I wasn't aware you knew my squadron leader." He glanced at his watch. "Sam hadn't returned when I left the base. If he's back in his quarters by the time I'm finished here, I'll request that he take you home."

Polly's face was transformed by her smile. "Thank you, sir. Much obliged, I'm sure." She backed out of the door, still beaming.

Earl shook his head. "I hope this doesn't break any of your rules?"

"Not at all." Elizabeth reached for her champagne glass. "Things have changed so much since I was a young girl. Servants have so much more freedom nowadays, and I'm afraid they have become lax in their duties as well as their attitudes. I'm not sure it's a good thing. One can't even refer to them as servants anymore without offending them."

"War changes a lot of things." Earl looked around the vast room with appreciation. "It's good that you're not close to a big city. It would be a crime to lose a place like this to a bomb. It must be hundreds of years old."

"Seventeenth century, actually." Elizabeth followed his gaze to the ornate ceiling, lovingly etched by ancient hands. "I just hope we can escape the bombs for the rest of the war. Norwich isn't that far away, and it was heavily bombed in April of this year. I'm afraid the Norfolk coast can be quite vulnerable to attack, especially from the sea. We are all supposed to carry gas masks with us all the time, though it's mostly the children who carry them these days."

"Well, I reckon you're well protected with a British army camp and an American Army Air Force base in the area."

"As well as mined beaches and barbed wire along the cliffs. Not to mention Rita Crumm and her gallant troops," Elizabeth murmured.

Earl looked intrigued. "Sorry?"

"Just a misguided, though very enthusiastic, group of

housewives with an overambitious female tyrant for a leader."

Earl grinned. "I take it you don't care for this Rita person?"

She made a face at him. "Rita means well, I suppose, but she can be incredibly tiresome at times. I make allowances for them all. It must be hard to sit twiddling their thumbs while their husbands are risking their lives in a foreign land. Playing at soldiers makes them feel useful, as if they are doing their bit. And most of them do a lot for the war effort, like knitting woollies for the winter, collecting scrap metal, working in victory gardens, that sort of thing. Right now they have organized a massive clothes drive in the village, to help the people who have been bombed out of their homes."

The major looked impressed. "Tell me about the murder. Was it really a land girl with her head chopped off?"

"Not exactly. It *was* one of the land girls, unfortunately, but as far as I know, her head was still intact. She was brutally attacked, however, with an axe, so the constables tell me."

"And the police think the German pilot killed her?"

Elizabeth pursed her lips. "They don't really know who killed her yet."

"And what do you think?"

She studied her glass for a moment or two before answering. "I think," she said slowly, "that there are a lot more questions to be answered before we can even begin to discover what really happened." Questions she would somehow have to take care of herself, she silently added, if true justice was to be served.

CHAPTER
7

Elizabeth was well pleased with the meal that Violet served up that evening, helped somewhat by Martin under the housekeeper's eagle eye. Violet had managed to find a small beef roast, and the Yorkshire puddings definitely had been made with an egg—a vast improvement on the heavy lumps of batter everyone had been forced to endure for the past months.

The sherry trifle was a delight, delicate and flavorful as it should be. In fact, it tasted so good Elizabeth wondered if Violet had recruited a friend of hers to make it—a thought she would have to keep to herself for fear of insulting her housekeeper.

Earl was excellent company, amusing her with stories of his hometown in Wyoming—a place called Rock Springs, which, according to Earl, wasn't much bigger than Sitting Marsh. Yet from the way he described the vast open lands surrounding it, there was a whole world of difference in his life there.

How he must miss it all, she thought as she listened to him talk about rodeos, roundups, and so many other things beyond her imagination. It was a magical world he talked about, and in spite of her good intentions, she envied the woman who waited for him to return.

Violet served brandy in the conservatory, obviously flattered by Earl's effusive praise of her cooking. Even Elizabeth had to admit Violet had outdone herself and made a mental note to tell her so at the first opportunity.

Alone with the major, she did her best to relax in front of the glass walls that overlooked the lawns. This was her favorite room in the house—her own special sanctuary—and Earl Monroe was one of the few people she had allowed in her haven. She often wondered what he would make of that if she were to tell him so.

Settled on the wicker chairs, they chatted about the history of the Manor House, until he surprised her by asking, "Don't you think it's time you told me what it was you wanted to discuss?"

She tried to remember what it was that had seemed so important that morning. "There was really nothing specific," she admitted at last. "I was wondering if you had any concerns about your accommodations and if there was anything any of us could do to make you more comfortable. You must be rather cramped up there."

"I don't think the men mind that at all." Earl set down his empty brandy glass. "It's a heck of a lot better than anything on base, and they get a kick out of staying in a big old house like this. They call it the Palace."

"Really." She rather liked that, Elizabeth decided. "You must let me know if you get too cold. I'm afraid the only source of heating is the fireplace, but we have plenty of coal in the cellar for fires, and I can tell Polly to make them up for you in the mornings."

"It's not that cold yet. I reckon the only thing that keeps the men awake at night is the noise in the water pipes. Sometimes it sounds like a freight train going through a tunnel."

Elizabeth sighed. "I know what you mean. Dreadful noise. The plumbing is so ancient in this house. I should have someone look at it."

"I can ask around the base if you like. I reckon I can find a plumber among the guys out there. Give him a home-cooked meal like the one I had tonight and he'll be happy to help out."

Delighted, Elizabeth beamed at him. "Would you? That is really most kind of you."

"Least I can do after dumping my men in your home."

"Oh, but that wasn't your fault."

"No, ma'am. Doesn't make it any easier on you or your servants, though."

"Oh, they don't mind, really. Violet loves to take care of people, and Polly thinks she's in paradise now that she's surrounded by Americans. Even Martin seems to have brightened up since you arrived. Things have been rather dull around here for him since my parents died."

"I wouldn't say a murder is dull, Lady Elizabeth."

She took a moment to answer him. She liked the way he said her name. It sounded softer, more romantic somehow, when he said it. Pulling herself together, she said a little more sharply than she'd intended, "Maybe not, but I'd just as soon do without it."

"I'm sure you would. I didn't mean—"

"I know you didn't." She rose, bringing him to his feet as well. "I'm sorry, Major Monroe. I'm a little tired, I suppose."

He gave her one of his piercing stares. "You're not involved in this murder business again?"

"Not really." She shivered and rubbed her upper arms with her hands. "Though murder in a village the size of Sitting Marsh is thoroughly unsettling to everyone. Somehow I can't help feeling a little sorry for that young German, hunted down by soldiers and the police, alone in a strange, hostile country where he doesn't even know the language."

"He'd shoot you as soon as look at you, and from what I've heard, seems he hacked a young girl to death with an axe."

"I know." She did her best to summon a smile. "I'm being far too sentimental, I admit. It's just as well I'm not a policewoman. I would take it all far too personally."

He returned her smile. "I reckon they could do a lot worse."

"Thank you." Flustered, she moved to the door. "Goodnight, Major. I've enjoyed talking to you. Please, let me know if there's anything else my staff or I can do for you."

He hesitated, opened his mouth as if to say something, then closed it again. "Goodnight, Lady Elizabeth."

Her curiosity would not let it go. "You were going to say something?"

He shrugged, looking embarrassed. "Well, it's kind of weird, I guess, and I'm sure there's some simple explanation . . ."

His voice trailed off, and she waited, intrigued by his hesitancy. When he didn't immediately continue, she said impatiently, "Major Monroe, if something is not acceptable in the east wing, I trust you would tell me."

"There's probably nothing to it."

"Nothing to what?"

"Well, this is going to sound real crazy, but some of my men have talked about seeing something in the grand hallway. I was just wondering if you had some kind of explanation I could give them."

Remembering Martin's muttering about her father's ethereal return to the Manor House, she felt a chill of apprehension. "You mean the great hall? What did they see?"

"The great hall. Yes, ma'am. Well, a couple of the men swear they saw . . . a ghost."

She felt as if all her breath had been cut off. "That's ridiculous," she said faintly.

"That's what I told them, ma'am."

"It must have been a shadow or something. These old houses can play dreadful tricks on the eyes."

He nodded, his gaze grave on her face. "I couldn't agree more."

She allowed a few seconds to slip by then said briskly, "Well, I'm glad we got that settled."

"So am I. Thank you for a swell evening. Please give my regards to the chef. The meal was excellent."

"I'm glad you enjoyed it, Major." She watched him leave with the feeling that they hadn't really settled anything at all. A ghost. Was it possible Martin hadn't been entirely imagining things after all? *Wonderful.* That's all she needed now, on top of everything else.

It was several minutes later before she remembered that they hadn't settled the matter of Polly's lift home. She rang the bell to the kitchen and waited for what seemed an eternity for someone to answer. When the door finally opened, it was Martin who poked his head into the room.

"You rang, madam?"

"It's late, Martin. Why aren't you in bed?"

"I have no idea, madam. Why aren't I in bed?"

"Are you helping Violet with something?"

"No, madam. Violet has retired for the evening."

"What about Polly? Has she left?"

"Yes, madam. I believe she was in the company of an American."

Relieved that Polly had been taken care of, Elizabeth nodded. "Martin, do try to remove that tone of disgust from your voice when you mention the Americans."

"Yes, madam."

"And I suggest you also retire for the evening."

"Very well, madam."

He'd sounded a little distant, and Elizabeth narrowed her eyes. "Do I sense a note of disapproval?"

Martin raised his chin. "It is not for me to pass judgement on your social activities, madam."

"Indeed not, Martin. I should hope the thought never crossed your mind."

"I should merely like to point out that the master is displeased."

"Really. Well, tell the master that I'm in charge here now, and what I do is my own business."

"He won't like that, madam."

"Quite possibly, but nevertheless, it happens to be the truth. And I fail to see what he can do about it now." *Great heavens!* she thought. She was talking as if her father were still alive. She really needed to get some sleep. As for all this talk about ghosts, there had to be a simple explanation. She would investigate the great hall herself tomorrow and put all these silly rumors to rest.

Polly bounced down hard on the seat as the Jeep lurched across a bump in the lane. She made the most of the opportunity and swayed hard against Sam's arm.

"Sorry," he said, looking not in the least sorry about it. "Didn't see that one coming."

"It's all right." She tried to think of something clever to say, but her mind had gone completely blank. "I'm sorry I couldn't meet you down the pub tonight. I had to work late. Thank you for taking me home, anyhow."

"It's my pleasure, believe me." He jammed his foot on the brake as they approached the crossroads then swept around the corner, ending up on the wrong side of the road.

"You're on the wrong side again," Polly reminded him. "You Yanks will never get the hang of driving on the right side of the road."

"I thought we were supposed to drive on the left side of the road."

She nudged him. "Go on, you know what I mean."

He pulled over to the left, bringing them up close to

the edge of the woods. "I'm sure glad you're not out here riding your bike at this time of night. How come you're so late, anyhow? Do all secretaries work this late in England?"

Guiltily she crossed her fingers. "Nah, it's just that this was a special night for Lady Elizabeth, and Violet asked me to help out."

"Yeah, what goes on with the major and her ladyship? They got something going?"

Polly laughed. " 'Course not. The major's married, anyhow. Violet told me. Lady Elizabeth would never have anything to do with a married man. Nor would I." She looked up at Sam's handsome face, stricken by the thought that just crossed her mind. "You're not married, are you?"

Sam snorted. "Me? Not on your pretty little life, sweetheart. I'm too fond of my freedom to get hitched."

Well satisfied, Polly leaned back in her seat. She'd change all that, she promised herself. It would just take a little time, that was all. From the first moment she'd set eyes on Captain Sam Cutter, she'd made up her mind that she was going to marry him and go back to America with him, and nothing was going to stop her.

"Makes me nervous, knowing there's a Nazi hiding in those woods," Sam muttered as the Jeep roared down the lane.

Polly sniffed the night air. She loved the smell of the woods at night, especially now that autumn was here turning the trees to red and gold and ripening scarlet berries all over the holly boughs. Even the thought of a murderer lurking among the silent trees couldn't dampen her spirits. She was alone with the man of her dreams, and in a few moments he'd be kissing her goodnight outside her house.

She'd make it last as long as possible, she silently vowed, because the sooner Sam fell in love with her, the sooner she could tell him the truth about her age. In a few months she'd be sixteen and old enough to work in the factory. Then she could buy lots of fancy clothes and shoes and perfume and makeup, and she wouldn't have to worry about skulking around the Manor House, frightened someone would see her cleaning the loo.

"There was a big fight in the pub tonight," Sam said as they pulled out onto the coast road. "The British army were there and got into a brawl with our boys."

Polly gasped. "You weren't hurt, were you?"

"Nope. We got out as soon as it started, but judging from the noise going on in there, I bet there were a few bloody noses and black eyes."

"Oh, my. I bet Ted Wilkins was fit to be tied. He keeps threatening to shut down the pub if they keep having fights in there."

"Well, I reckon it was worse than usual because of all the army boys in town looking for the murderer."

"They still haven't found him yet, then?"

"Doesn't seem like it." He sent Polly a sideways glance that thrilled her to bits. "Can't say I'm sorry if it gives me an excuse to take a gorgeous dame like you home."

His words made her sigh. He'd called her gorgeous. He made her feel like a real woman. She knew what it was like now, to be really in love. Not like those silly little crushes she'd had on the English boys. They all seemed so childish now. Now that she had a real man to love. Hugging herself, she leaned closer to him, tingling with the anticipation of his goodnight kiss.

Sleep eluded Elizabeth until the early hours of the morning, and when she did finally drift off, her dreams disturbed her with images of a headless woman chasing German soldiers through the woods.

Her lack of sleep made her feel out of sorts as she made her way down to the kitchen that morning, and the news that the British army had spent the entire night combing the woods without finding any trace of the German pilot did nothing to settle her brittle nerves. Violet, who had heard the news from Polly, also informed her that Rita Crumm was rounding up her troops to hunt for the escaped pilot.

"They're supposed to meet at the village green at ten this morning," Violet said, putting a steaming plate of porridge in front of Elizabeth. "Polly's mother's going with them."

Elizabeth looked at her in alarm. "Someone could get badly hurt with all those soldiers searching the woods."

"I'd worry about the soldiers if I were you. Polly said the women will be carrying butcher knives."

"That's got to be illegal. Someone has to stop them before things get out of hand."

"Seems to me things are already getting out of hand. Ooh, that's something else Polly told me." Violet went to the door and stuck her head into the hallway. "Martin!" she yelled. "Your porridge is ready!" She came back shaking her head. "That man. I swear he's going deaf."

"I'd be surprised if he wasn't. After all, he's in his eighties. Something's bound to wear out at that age."

"If you ask me, it's his blinking mind that's wearing out," Violet muttered. "He keeps nattering on about the master being back. He's giving me the willies now."

Remembering the major's words, Elizabeth decided it was time to change the subject. "What was it that Polly told you?"

Violet picked up a large wooden spoon and stirred the rest of the porridge. "There was a big fight down at the pub last night. Our lads and the Yanks got into it, according to Polly. Made a right mess of the place before it was over."

Elizabeth stared at her plate. "We have to do something about that. I think I'll call a meeting of the town council. Perhaps we can come up with some ideas of how to end this resentment of the Americans."

"It's going to take more than a council meeting to do that if you ask me." Violet ladled porridge into a bowl.

"At least this time they can't blame the murder on a Yank." She carried the bowl over to the table and set it down. "I wonder what Rita Crumm and her lot would do if they came across that German."

"Probably run for their lives," Martin said from the doorway. "That's if they've got any sense. That blighter would run them through with a bayonet if they got anywhere near him."

"He's not carrying a bayonet," Elizabeth remarked. She lifted a spoonful of porridge in the air. "He must be pretty hungry by now."

"Not thinking of taking him your porridge, are you?" Violet asked as she filled a third bowl with the oatmeal.

Martin gasped. "I should say not! I would hope madam has far too much prudence than to consider such a dangerous venture."

"Madam does," Elizabeth assured him. "I was just wondering if the poor boy is hungry enough to give himself up."

"That poor boy killed a young woman, so stop feeling sorry for him," Violet said, seating herself at the table. She looked up at Martin, who hovered by his chair. "Are you going to sit down, or are you waiting for your porridge to get cold first?"

Martin cleared his throat. "May I have your permission to join you at the table, madam?"

Elizabeth answered automatically. "You may, Martin."

"Thank you, madam, but if I may say so, your proper place is in the dining room at the dining room table. The master is very unhappy to see how badly proprieties have been neglected at the Manor House."

"Then I should think he was delirious last night," Violet said crisply. "Especially when you nearly dropped the soup all over Lizzie. If you ask me, she's a lot safer right here in the kitchen."

Martin was too busy concentrating on getting his creaking body down on his chair to answer her.

Elizabeth glanced at her. "How did you know about the soup?"

"I was watching from the doorway, wasn't I. The old fool insisted on taking it in, and I was holding my breath all the way. I nearly had a heart attack when I saw it slipping, until your major caught it."

Elizabeth frowned. "Once and for all, Violet, he's not *my* major, and I do wish you would stop calling him that."

"Methinks you do protest too much," Violet murmured.

Ignoring her, Elizabeth cleared her plate, then laid down her spoon. "I have to go down to the police station this morning. Would you ring the council members for me and have them meet me at the town hall at half past two this afternoon?"

"I'll get Polly to do it. She likes using the telephone." She tilted her head to one side. "You know, I've been thinking, maybe you should give some thought to her helping out in the office after all. With all the running about you've been doing lately, it must be hard for you to keep up with all the accounting."

Surprised, Elizabeth rose to her feet. "Has she been talking to you about it?"

Martin painfully pulled himself up out of his chair, while Violet gulped down a spoonful of porridge. "Never shuts up about it. I'm tired of listening to her."

"Did she ask you to mention it to me?"

"I sort of promised I'd say something." Violet looked up at her. "Not that I'm saying you should take her on, of course. I don't want to be blamed if she messes everything up."

Elizabeth sat down again. "I suppose I could use some help in the office."

Martin, who had frozen midway in his effort to rise, lowered himself on the chair.

"Well, it's up to you, Lizzie. I'm not the one to tell you what to do."

"Does she have any experience?"

Violet shrugged. "Not that I know of, but she seems intelligent enough to learn. You'd probably have to be behind her at first, but I think she'd do all right. It would get her off my back with her whining all the time."

"Well, I'll think about it." Elizabeth got to her feet once more. "Though she'll still have to find time to clean the house."

Martin sighed, then struggled off his chair.

"She'll have plenty of time," Violet assured her. "She doesn't have enough to occupy her now, and working in the office would stop her from hanging around the east wing all the time. She's too blinking young to be running after men. Especially hot-blooded ones like those Yanks."

"I say, Violet," Martin protested.

"Well, we don't have the right to supervise her private life." Elizabeth looked at Martin. "You can sit down now, Martin. I'm leaving."

"Yes, madam," Martin murmured, remaining on his feet.

"I take it you enjoyed your dinner last night with your major," Violet said slyly.

On her way to the door, Elizabeth paused. "Oh, I'm sorry, Violet, I meant to tell you how much we both enjoyed the meal. You surpassed yourself last night. Especially the trifle. It was quite your best effort ever."

Violet looked immensely pleased with herself. "Glad to hear it, Lizzie. Only the best for you, that's what I say."

Elizabeth escaped through the door, before Violet's questions could get any more personal. She didn't want to talk about last night to anyone. It had been a special evening and hers to keep in her memory forever.

Right now, however, she had more serious thoughts to dwell on. There was the problem of the hostility in the village toward the Americans that had to be resolved. Even more pressing was the murder case, which was why she was anxious to get down to the police station as soon as possible. Someone had to stop Rita Crumm and her troops before the search for the German ended in more tragedy.

CHAPTER

✿ 8 ✿

Both George and Sid were seated in the front office of the police station when Elizabeth arrived there a short while later. A light shower had dampened her Panama hat on the way, leaving the brim drooping dismally over one eye. The wet skirt of her wool dress flapped around her knees as she strode over to the desk, reminding her that there were definite disadvantages to utilizing a motorcycle as one's sole mode of transportation.

All in all, she was not in her best mood when George greeted her in his usual brusque tones. "Morning, Lady Elizabeth! What can we do for you today?"

"You can put a stop to Rita Crumm's ridiculous endeavor to get herself and her friends shot and killed, that's what you can do." Elizabeth sat down rather hard on the rickety chair in front of the desk.

Sid came over to stand next to George. "What she's doing now then, m'm?"

"She's taking her foolish little followers into the woods to hunt for that German pilot, knowing full well that the military is in there ready to shoot at anything that's not wearing army boots and battledress."

Sid tutted, and George shook his head. "Rita means well," he muttered, "but she does get a little heavy-handed at times."

"Means well? Is that all you can say?" Aware that she was sputtering, Elizabeth made an effort to sound more ladylike. "I insist that you do something to stop her. Someone could very well get killed out there."

Sid nodded but obviously had nothing helpful to offer.

George looked worried. "Begging your pardon, Lady Elizabeth, but we can't stop people going into the woods if they have a mind to go. It's not like it's private property or anything."

"I'm perfectly aware of that. Since it is part of the Manor House estate, however, I can ask that you deem the area out of bounds until the pilot has been captured or the search has been called off."

Sid nodded again then changed it to shaking negatively when George murmured, "I'm not sure we can do that, m'm. The first Lord Hartleigh made it very clear that the entire village and the surrounding lands, with the exception of the Manor House grounds, were to remain open and accessible to all residents of Sitting Marsh. No matter what. He signed and sealed it a hundred years ago. It's hanging right up there on the wall of the town hall. Your own father was very protective of that law, if I remember rightly."

Elizabeth gritted her teeth. Why was it that lately everywhere she turned the specter of her father loomed in front of her? "I'm well aware of my great-great-grandfather's decree, George. However, a hundred years ago I doubt very much if he envisioned young men, most of them recovering from a drunken brawl, running around the woods with rifles using helpless housewives for target practice. I must insist that you take some action to prevent a possible disaster."

George tapped a pencil on his blotter with maddening deliberation, while Sid looked sorrowful, reminding Elizabeth of a basset hound she'd almost purchased a while ago.

Finally George said heavily, "I suppose I could have a word with them."

"I don't think a word is going to stop Rita Crumm. You know how she is when she hears the call to battle. She takes up arms and charges into the fray like some inept Viking."

"It's all I have the authority to do, m'm. Until they do something unlawful, anyway."

Elizabeth lifted her chin. "What if I were to tell you that they will be carrying carving knives with them?"

Sid gasped, while George looked alarmed. "Carving knives? Are you sure about this, m'm?"

"Well, no, not first hand," Elizabeth had to admit. "Polly told Violet, who told me. But I'm sure—"

"Begging your pardon again, m'm, but I can't see how I can arrest people even if they are carrying a knife. Not without murderous intent, that is."

Elizabeth curled her fingers into her palms. "George, they are not going on a picnic. Why else would they carry knives?"

"To protect themselves? These are dangerous times after all, what with a murdering Nazi running around the woods. Then there's the rest of his crew. What happened to them? What if they met up with our bloke, and now there's a crowd of them out there, all gunning for us? We could all be stiff'uns before the day is out."

"God save us all," Sid muttered, clutching his chest.

Elizabeth had to admit she hadn't thought of that. "All the more reason you should stop Rita before she takes those fools into the woods," she snapped.

"That's as may be, m'm, but if Mrs. Crumm is determined to spend the day in the woods with her friends, there isn't a whole lot I can do about it. My advice is to just let them be."

She glared at him in frustration. How someone could manage to look like a saintly monk yet be so infuriating was beyond her. "George, if I didn't know better, I'd say you were afraid of tackling Rita Crumm."

"When it comes down to facing a bunch of hysterical women armed with bread knives, m'm, I'd say that a certain amount of prudence is called for," George said carefully.

"Carving knives, George. There's a difference."

"Yes, m'm."

"Lady Elizabeth's right, George," Sid said eagerly. "My Ethel's bread knife has got little jagged edges on it, but the carving knife is bigger, and it's got a strai—"

"I know what a bloody carving knife looks like," George growled, "so pipe down Sid, and let me take care of this." He glanced up at Elizabeth. "Please excuse us, m'm."

"You're excused." Elizabeth folded her gloved hands in her lap. Obviously, as usual, she would have to take care of Rita and her troops herself. Abandoning the subject, she said tersely, "What about that army lieutenant, Jeff Thomas? Have you spoken to him?"

"Yes, m'm, I have." George's expression suggested he was doing his best to humor a particularly trying client. "Lieutenant Thomas has not left the base for the past week. He's in quarantine in the sick bay. Chicken pox, I believe."

Elizabeth straightened in her chair. Then obviously it wasn't Jeff Thomas who was arguing with Amelia the other night. So who had spent the evening with the dead girl? Who had argued with her late at night beneath Sheila's window? Could it have been Maurice after all?

Feeling disheartened, Elizabeth asked, "Did you question Sheila Macclesby yesterday?"

George's face seemed to close up. "I'm not at liberty to say at this time, m'm."

She leaned forward. "George, I'll be seeing her sooner or later. She'll tell me if you were out there."

"Well, I suppose I can say that I was at the farmhouse, yes."

"You can say you talked to her," Sid said helpfully and received a glare for his efforts.

"Did you happen to question her son?" Elizabeth gave Sid an encouraging smile. Sometimes she learned more from Sid's artless comments than from all of George's ponderous reports.

"I spoke to him, yes." George frowned. "For all the good it did. Wouldn't say a word."

"He's not right in the head, m'm," Sid put in. "That's why he won't talk."

"I wish *you* wouldn't bloody talk quite so much." George glanced at Elizabeth. "Pardon me again, m'm."

Elizabeth nodded. "What about the land girls? Did you talk to them?"

"Yes, m'm, I did." George put his pencil down and leaned back in his chair. "I don't wish to be discourteous, Lady Elizabeth, but if you ask me, all this questioning is nothing but a waste of time. We're pretty sure this German bloke did it, and when we catch him we'll prove it."

"But what if he didn't? What if someone else killed Amelia? All the time you are chasing after the German, the real murderer could be free to kill again or at the very least have time to cover his tracks. We have to consider all possibilities, George. We can't just assume someone's guilt because they happen to be in the vicinity."

"Lady Elizabeth," George began speaking very slowly and clearly, as if explaining something to an infant, "there are three things that a constable takes into account in a murder case." He held up his fingers one by one.

"One, there's motive. Two, there's opportunity. Three, there's alibi."

Containing her irritation with remarkable constraint, Elizabeth said quietly, "As far as the German is concerned, there appears to be only one of the three you can count on—opportunity. But without the murder weapon you have no proof of anything. Have you found the axe yet?"

"No, m'm, we haven't, but that doesn't prove anything. According to the medical examiner, the victim was killed very late at night, and the body was then moved to its final destination. Since we have no way of knowing exactly where the victim was killed, we don't know where to start looking for the axe."

"That's *if* she was killed with an axe," Sid added.

Elizabeth snapped her gaze to his face. "There's some doubt of that?"

Sid nodded. "The doctor doesn't think it were an axe that split her head open. He thinks the Nazi hit her with some kind of garden tool with a blunt edge. Like a hoe or a spade."

George sent a scathing glance at Sid. "That was supposed to be confidential information."

"Sorry," Sid muttered.

"Makes no difference." George sighed. "Since we know the victim wasn't actually killed in the woods, the German must have killed her somewhere else, then carried her into the woods after she was dead. Wherever he killed her, that's where the murder weapon will be. He could have armed himself with a hoe or spade from any of the farms around here. Or any houses, come to that."

"But most likely at the Macclesby farm," Elizabeth said dryly, "considering that's where the victim lived and had presumably arrived home late that night. Not to mention she was heard arguing with someone there. I should think that would be fairly obvious."

George looked offended. "Naturally I conducted a search of the premises, and there were several tools in the vicinity. None of which appeared to have been used as a murder weapon."

Elizabeth didn't answer. She was remembering Maisie's missing spade that turned up later in the tool-shed. If Amelia was killed at the Macclesby farm, it appeared more and more as if Maurice might be involved. On the other hand, there were also the questions of who had kept Amelia company on her last evening on earth and where she had spent her final hours.

"None of the tools I looked at," George said, "had any signs of damage or bloodstains. That doesn't mean the Nazi didn't take it with him, to keep as a weapon. Then again, he could have found it anywhere. Then again, we don't know for certain that the young lady was killed at the Macclesby farm."

Elizabeth glanced at the large clock above George's head. If she was going to talk Rita Crumm out of her foolhardy expedition, she had to leave now. Since both George and Sid seemed convinced the German pilot had committed the murder, there was no point in wasting her time or theirs until she had more information. In the meantime, she had a group of imprudent housewives to save.

"Well, I'll pop in tomorrow to see if you have any more news," she said, rising from her chair. "In the meantime, I'd appreciate it if you would call me if there are any further developments. My housemaid has to cycle home past those woods. I'd like to know when the German is captured so that I no longer have to be concerned for her safety."

"I'll be sure that you get the message, m'm," George said, stumbling to his feet. "Thank you for stopping by."

"Not at all, George. Thank you for answering my questions."

"Yes, well, you can thank Sid for most of that." The unfortunate Sid received another baleful glare. "Oh, I almost forgot. The victim's parents are driving down today to claim the body. I thought you'd want to know."

"Thank you, George. I trust you can take care of that?"

"Of course, m'm. No need to worry on that account. Just one word of warning, though, if I may. I'd steer clear of Mrs. Crumm and her brood. Never know what she'll be up to next, but one thing I do know, she's quite capable of taking care of herself."

"I'm sure she is," Elizabeth said as she headed for the door, "but it's not Rita I'm worried about. It's all those empty-headed, trusting fools who plunge joyfully into jeopardy behind her."

She left the warmth of the station and climbed aboard her motorcycle. Although the rain had ceased, she could feel a distinct nip in the air. The smell of dried grass and corn stubble had given way to the pungent aroma of seaweed and salt. The winds had shifted. Soon the nights would be drawing in, and morning frost would coat the bare branches of the oaks and beech trees in the woods. Already the prickly burrs were falling from the chestnut trees, and the children would be gathering them to roast in the fireplaces.

Elizabeth secured her hat by tying her scarf under her chin. She hoped fervently that mothers would make every effort to keep their children out of the woods until the German was captured and the murder solved. Time was of the essence, and it seemed unlikely she would receive much help from the local constabulary.

There wasn't much she could do about capturing the German pilot, she acknowledged, as she sailed down the High Street with her skirt tucked up beneath her as much as modesty allowed. But she had managed to solve one murder without too much help from the police. There was no reason why she couldn't do it again.

She arrived at the village green just as Rita Crumm climbed up on the small pavilion, prepared to address her enthusiastic, if misguided, band of followers.

The roar of Elizabeth's motorcycle momentarily distracted the excited group, and several women turned to wave at her as she coasted to a halt.

Obviously put out by this unwarranted interruption, Rita screeched at the top of her lungs, "Ladies! Pay attention! We are here to serve our country today. So please stop nattering like magpies and listen to me."

Chatting busily, the women ignored her.

Elizabeth cut the engine, and in the deafening silence that followed, Rita bellowed, "I said, will you bloody fools listen to me!"

The women stopped talking. A couple of them giggled and were immediately nudged into silence by others.

"That's better." Rita tossed her head, and the little tight curls on her forehead bounced up and down. "This is serious. If we are going to hunt down a German we have to do it"—she raised her voice and yelled—"*quietly.*"

"You tell 'em, Ma!" a high-pitched voice encouraged from the front of the crowd.

Elizabeth recognized Rita's daughter, Lilly, who had apparently taken a day off from the factory to join in the hunt. The stupidity of this woman in placing her own child in jeopardy astounded Elizabeth. Rita, however, seemed just as shocked to see her daughter standing there.

"Why aren't you at work?" she demanded.

"I've come to help you find that murdering bugger, haven't I," Lilly declared in a close emulation of her mother's strident voice.

"Over my dead body," Rita snapped back. "You get your blinking arse back to work this minute. I never heard of such a thing, taking off like that. You could lose your job over this."

"I wish." Lilly stuck her fingers into her muddy blond hair and fluffed up the curls. "They're not going to sack me, Ma . . . they need all the help they can get down there."

"I don't care if they sack you or not. You're going back there this minute."

"Aw, Ma . . . I want to help you find that Nazi. I even brought a knife with me."

Sunlight glinted on the blade of a wicked-looking butcher knife in Lilly's hand. A woman standing close to the young girl screamed.

"Shut up, you silly cow," Lilly muttered.

"You tell her, Lil," someone else called out.

Rita's face had turned crimson. "This is a job for grown women," she howled, "not children! Go back to work, Lilly, or I'll lock you in your bedroom when I get home."

"I'm not a child!" Lilly yelled back. "I'm seventeen. If I'm old enough to die from a bomb falling on me, I'm old enough to hunt down the bugger what's dropping them, so there!"

"Here, here! Yay!" The women clapped and cheered.

"Let's find the bugger and kill him!" someone else called out.

A roar of approval went up from the crowd.

Deciding it was time she intervened, Elizabeth stepped forward. A path miraculously cleared through the crowd in front of her. Amid murmured greetings, which she acknowledged with a gracious nod, she headed for the pavilion.

Rita watched her approach, her grim expression warning Elizabeth that she had no easy task in front of her. She climbed the worn steps of the pavilion and reached Rita's side.

"Lady Elizabeth," Rita muttered, her lips so thinned the words barely slipped through. "What a surprise. Have you come to join us in the hunt?"

"Certainly not." Elizabeth turned to face the crowd and raised her voice. "Listen to me, all of you. The military has sent soldiers to search the woods for the German pilot. If you go in there today you could very well be mistaken for him, and someone could get badly hurt. Please, go home and let the soldiers do their job."

"They need our help out there," Rita declared, addressing the housewives, who were muttering to each other again. "We know those woods better than any soldier. We know where to look."

"And what will you do when you find him?" Elizabeth demanded. "He's not going to understand anything you say."

"He'll understand this." Rita brandished a carving knife in her face.

The crowd sent up a few half-hearted cheers. "I don't want to hurt no one," someone said. "I faint at the sight of blood."

"Blood!" someone else exclaimed. "No one said anything about no blood!"

"We're not going to use the knives!" Rita wailed. "They are just to frighten him, that's all."

"Can't we frighten him with our fists?" someone asked.

"What fists?" her neighbor demanded. "I ain't got no fists."

"I'm going home," someone else called out. "I don't want to be shot at by no soldiers."

A chorus of "me neither" greeted the woman's announcement.

Ignoring Rita's frantic pleas, the housewives began drifting off, one by one, until only three remained, one of whom was Lilly.

"You still here?" Rita punched her fists into her hips. "I thought I told you to go back to work."

"I'm going," Lilly mumbled. "It's more fun there than standing here watching a bunch of old biddies wetting their drawers at the thought of being shot at. Blinking good job they're not in the real army. We'd lose the bloody war."

"Watch your bloody language in front of Lady Elizabeth!" Rita shouted.

"Sorry, m'm," Lilly hunched her shoulders and

grabbed the bicycle she'd leaned against the wall of the abandoned sweet shop. "Better watch out if you go in the woods, Ma. One look at your face, and that Nazi'll run all the way back to Germany." She swung a leg across the saddle in a most inelegant manner that would have been embarrassing were it not for the fact that she wore slacks. "Ta ta for now!" With a last defiant wave of her hand she wobbled off down the lane.

"You must excuse my daughter, Lady Elizabeth," Rita said, her face flushed as red as a beetroot. "She's going through that age, you know."

Not quite certain as to what exactly "that age" referred to, Elizabeth smiled instead. She was so immensely relieved that a potentially dangerous situation had been successfully defused she felt like beaming at everyone. Even Rita Crumm. "I'm so glad you all changed your minds," she said.

"Oh, I think you deserve the credit for changing their minds, Lady Elizabeth," Rita said, ice forming on her words. "I do hope the soldiers have better luck in finding that murderer today. I should hate for someone else to be killed because they didn't have enough people out there looking for him."

Although she refused to let Rita see it, Elizabeth felt a strong pang of apprehension. She felt perfectly justified in persuading the women not to go into the woods. As far as the murderer was concerned, however, she couldn't help feeling she wasn't doing everything she could to find out who had killed Amelia Brunswick.

What was even more disturbing, she couldn't rid herself of the notion that she already had the answer to the puzzle. It was buried so deeply in the recesses of her mind, however, that she could not bring it to the surface, no matter how she struggled. She could only hope for now that her fears were unfounded and that poor Maurice Macclesby had not hacked Amelia Brunswick to death with a spade.

CHAPTER
9

Elizabeth arrived home to the news that Sheila Macclesby had rung with an urgent message for her to call back.

"Sounded real upset, she did," Violet said, her wooden spoon swishing around in the vegetable soup she had boiling in the pot. "Wouldn't tell me what she wanted, though."

"I'll go up to the office and ring her after lunch." Elizabeth removed her gloves and sat down at the table. "Did you ring the council members?"

"Polly did. They'll all be at the town hall at half past two." Violet dished up a bowl of the soup and carried it over to the table. "Here, eat that. You look a bit frazzled."

Elizabeth ran a hand though her tangled locks. "It was that beastly shower this morning. It soaked my hat. I don't think it will ever be the same again."

"Panama hats are not supposed to be worn in the rain."

"It's the only decent one I have left beside the straw, and that's looking worse for wear now."

"There's a lot to be said for a good old-fashioned cloth pull-on, that's what I say." Violet placed another bowl of soup on the table.

Elizabeth wrinkled her nose. "They are so awfully drab. Not in the least bit fashionable."

"They're good enough for the queen. The king doesn't seem to mind her wearing them."

"I doubt if the king has much say in the matter," Elizabeth murmured. "Besides, royalty are supposed to wear hats without brims so that people can see their faces. The royal family has never been too adventurous when it comes to fashion, in any case. I wouldn't be caught dead in some of the clothes the queen wears."

"Elizabeth Hartleigh Compton! Watch your tongue! You shouldn't be talking about the royal family like that." Violet went to the door and yelled for Martin. "I don't know what he gets up to lately," she said, coming back to the table, "but he's never on time for meals anymore. He used to hover around the kitchen like a starving pigeon waiting for me to dish up, but now I have to call him down all the time."

"Martin doesn't have much sense of anything nowadays. He's living in the past most of the time."

"Don't I know it." Violet looked at the clock. "His soup is going to get cold if he doesn't hurry up. Where can he be?"

"He's probably talking to Father in the great hall," Elizabeth murmured, only half paying attention. Her mind was on the message from Sheila Macclesby. She'd deliberately put off calling her until after lunch because she was afraid Sheila was going to tell her that Maurice had killed Amelia and would then beg her to help him. If Maurice had killed the girl, there was absolutely nothing she could do about it. She wasn't looking forward to telling Sheila that.

She was startled when Violet said crossly, "Don't you start with this ghost business, Lizzie. I've had enough of it with Martin, and now Polly swears she saw something funny in the great hall. Wouldn't tell me what it was, but I could tell it shook her up. Martin I can see, but Polly usually has more sense than that. Mind you, what with all those pipes rattling every time someone goes to the lavatory, it's no wonder people start imagining things."

Elizabeth gradually became aware of what Violet was saying. She looked up sharply. "Polly saw a ghost?"

Violet shrugged. "I don't know that it was a ghost she saw, but she saw something odd, that I can tell you. 'Course, everyone knows there's no such things as ghosts, don't they?" She sent a nervous glance at Elizabeth. "Stuff and nonsense, that's what I say."

She didn't sound too convinced, and Elizabeth did her best to reassure her. "There are no such things as ghosts, Violet, so you can stop worrying."

Violet looked relieved. "I'm not worried at all." She peered up at the clock again. "Where *is* that man? I'll have to heat up his soup again." She picked up the bowl and returned the contents to the pot.

"I've finished mine," Elizabeth said, getting up from her chair. "I'll find him on my way up to the office and tell him his lunch is ready."

"His lunch is past ready," Violet said grimly. "It's on its way to the sink if he doesn't hurry up. By the way, you never told me how you got on at the police station. They haven't found that German yet, I suppose?"

"Not as far as I know." Elizabeth paused at the door. "They're still looking, of course. At least, the army is looking for him."

"I wonder if they've run across Rita and her lot yet."

"Rita and her troops had a change of heart about hunting down the German, lucky for him."

"Go on! Not like Rita to give up on a chance to glorify herself. Mind you, it's just as well. Anything could have happened with all those soldiers running around."

"That's exactly what I told them."

Violet tilted her head to one side. "I had an idea you might be responsible for them changing their minds."

"Someone had to do it, and the constables weren't too cooperative."

"Yes, but why does it always have to be you?" Violet wagged a finger at her. "You'll get yourself into more trouble than you can handle one of these fine days, Lizzie. You see if you don't."

Elizabeth smiled. "You worry too much, Violet. After all, it's my duty to watch over the villagers, and I'm very good at taking care of myself."

"No woman is good at taking care of herself. You need a man to do that."

"I tried that. Look where it landed me. If there's one thing I don't need in my life, it's another man." She left on those words, before Violet could give her any more argument.

It took her several minutes to find Martin. She finally spied him at the end of the great hall closest to the east wing. He stood at one of the tall, diamond-leaded windows, looking out at the neglected tennis court.

"He used to play there with your mother," Martin said when she reached his side.

Feeling a rush of warmth for the elderly man, she wished that protocol would allow her to give him a hug. There was not the slightest doubt in her mind that had she done so, Martin would probably faint dead away at the outrage. "I know," she said gently. "Both my parents loved to play tennis."

"No one plays on the tennis court now."

"Well, it's not very serviceable right now. The net is broken, and the grass needs cutting and marking again."

"He wants it repaired and spruced up."

She looked at him in surprise. "Who does?"

"The master, of course. He was just here, telling me so. I think he misses playing tennis."

Elizabeth glanced down the hall. It stretched the entire length of the house, and the far end was lost in shadows. Massive portraits of long-dead ancestors stared from their lofty perches on the walls with expressions varying from scowls to bored indifference. Not one of them smiled. If her portrait were to be hung alongside them, she would insist that she be smiling in it. No wonder people imagined they saw ghosts in such somber surroundings.

She looked the other way to the empty spaces still waiting. Her parents had sat for portraits shortly before their deaths. The massive paintings had been locked away for the past two years. She hadn't been able to bring herself to look at them. Now she couldn't remember if either of her parents had smiled in them. She would get them out, she decided, and have them hung where they belonged, alongside her grandparents, both of whom had passed away a few years ago. Her whole immediate family gone now. There were times when she felt like an orphan, left all alone in the world.

"Would you like me to see to it, madam?"

Jolted out of her thoughts, she stared at Martin. "See to what, Martin?"

"The tennis court, madam. I could spruce it up for the master."

"Oh, if you like." She eyed his frail body doubtfully. "Perhaps you can get Desmond to help. He's supposed to be taking care of the grounds."

Martin growled in his throat. "If you want my opinion madam, Desmond is about as useful in the grounds as a hole in an umbrella. I'll take care of the matter myself."

"As you wish." Remembering why she was there, she added quickly, "Oh, Martin, your soup is getting cold in the kitchen. You'd better hurry down there before Violet throws it out."

"Is it that time already?" Martin fumbled in his waistcoat pocket and drew out a large, silver pocket watch. "My word, where does the time go? If you'll excuse me, madam, I'll trot along to the kitchen now."

"Of course, Martin. Enjoy your lunch." She watched him shuffle slowly along the blue and gold carpet, his bowed figure frowned upon by the disdainful images on the walls. He had given his life to this house and the family who had lived there. If believing he could see the ghost of Lord Nigel Hartleigh made him happy, then who was she to deprive him of his fantasy?

She had almost reached her office when Polly came flying down the hallway, her long, black hair tumbling about her flushed face. In the old days, Elizabeth thought, no maid would be allowed into the main house without her hair pinned and tucked securely under her cap. Polly had absolutely refused to wear a cap. Times had changed indeed.

"Lady Elizabeth!" Fighting for breath, Polly halted in front of her.

Her clothes were at least halfway presentable today. The plaid skirt and white blouse were quite respectable, and so much more becoming than those dreadful slacks the young girls lived in nowadays. Elizabeth bestowed a smile on the young maid. "What can I do for you, Polly?"

"Well, m'm, I just wanted to tell you that I rang all those numbers Violet give me—"

"Gave me," Elizabeth corrected automatically.

"Sorry, m'm. Gave me. Anyhow, they all said as how they'd be at the meeting this afternoon. I got it all wrote down in a note on your desk."

Elizabeth generously ignored the further slip in grammar. "Thank you, Polly. I appreciate your efforts."

"Well, I was wondering, m'm, if you've given any more thought to me working in your office. I'm learning to talk proper now, and I'm getting really, really good at figures and writing letters, and I know I could manage all the bills. Violet showed me how to write out a check for the bank, so I know how to do that now, and I can answer the telephone and ring people and set up appointments and do all that for you."

Elizabeth frowned. She had to admit she could use the help, but she wasn't at all sure she could trust Polly with her varied and sometimes complicated duties. "I suppose I could use you for an hour every day," she said at last. "There's a mountain of filing to be done, and you could start there."

Polly nodded eagerly, her face wreathed in smiles. "I can do the filing, m'm. You just show me once, and I'll know how to do it."

Elizabeth sighed. "Very well, you can start tomorrow. Be in my office at half past eight."

"Yes, m'm." Polly poised to rush off.

"And Polly?"

"Yes, m'm?"

"You will still have to take care of the housework."

"Yes, m'm."

She had gone a few steps when Elizabeth stopped her again. "Oh, and Polly?"

This time the response came a little more warily. "Yes, m'm?"

"It's talk *properly*."

Polly grinned. "Yes, *ma'am!*"

The thoroughly American twang to the word made Elizabeth wince, but this time she let the young girl go. She had to ring Sheila Macclesby now to find out what was so urgent and she was dreading it.

Reaching her office, she sat down at the heavy oak desk and dialed the number of the farm. A young female voice answered her on the second ring, sounding breathless. "Macclesby farm!"

"This is Lady Elizabeth from the Manor House. I'd like to speak to Mrs. Macclesby, please."

"Oh, Lady Elizabeth! This is Pauline. Mrs. Macclesby's in the cowshed, trying to stop the soldiers from mucking about with the cows."

Elizabeth frowned. "What are soldiers doing in the cowshed?"

"They're looking for that German, that's what. He's been hiding in the barn. Maurice found some food up there, stolen from the kitchen. There was a scarf up there, too, with a swastika on it. He's not there now, though. I reckon he scarpered in the night."

While Elizabeth was still digesting the news, Pauline added, "Oh, wait a minute, here comes Mrs. Macclesby now!" There followed a babble of conversation too low for Elizabeth to hear, then Sheila Macclesby's clear voice rang in her ear.

"Good afternoon, your ladyship. Thank you for ringing. I just wanted you to know that Maurice found evidence that the German pilot has been hiding in our barn. The soldiers are looking for him now."

"So Pauline tells me. Is Maurice all right?"

"He's a little upset by all the excitement, but he's not hurt or anything. I wouldn't let the soldiers talk to him. You know how he gets. But at least now we know that the German killed Amelia. She must have seen him lurking around the farm, and he killed her to keep her quiet."

It was quite possible, Elizabeth had to admit. But then, if he'd killed to make good his escape, why would he go to all the trouble of dragging the body to the woods? "I have to go to a council meeting now," she told Sheila, "but as soon as it's over I'll come out there. Perhaps Maurice will feel more comfortable talking to me."

"I don't think he will, Lady Elizabeth. He won't talk to the constables and he knows them really well."

"George and Sid are there?"

"I think everyone in town is here," Sheila said, her exasperation sounding clearly in her voice. "Rita and her mob arrived a little while ago. They're all out in the fields looking in the haystacks. Don't know what they expect to find out there, but they are making a blooming mess, I can tell you. Begging your pardon, m'm."

"Oh dear." Elizabeth glanced at the small, pendulum

clock on her desk. "I'll be out there as soon as I can get there."

"Thank you, Lady Elizabeth. I need someone out here to take care of this mess. What with Rita Crumm and her lot, and the soldiers making trouble for the land girls, and all Sid and George can do is wander around wondering what to do next."

"I'll be there," Elizabeth promised and dropped the phone. The sooner she got the meeting over with, the sooner she could be out at the farm. Someone had to restore order out there before poor Sheila went out of her mind. Besides, she really wanted to talk to Maisie about the disappearing spade.

The other council members were already there when she arrived at the town hall a short while later. Deirdre Cumberland, the vicar's wife, dressed to kill as usual, was the first to greet her as she entered the dark, musty meeting room.

Returning the greeting, Elizabeth stepped up to the platform and took her seat at the head of the table. The acrid smell of burning tobacco wrinkled her nose. Captain Wally Carbunkle, long retired from the sea, puffed at a pipe while he listened to Percy Bodkins grumbling about all the extra accounts he had to deal with in his grocer's shop now that everything was on ration.

The fourth member of the council, a rotund, middle-aged woman whose red apple cheeks dimpled in a permanent smile, waved a hand at her from the opposite end of the table. "It's so nice to see you again, your ladyship," she called out. "How is poor old Martin getting along? All right, is he?"

"Thank you, yes, Bessie." Elizabeth smiled fondly at her. Bessie Bartholomew, proprietress and master baker at Bessie's Bake Shop, was always a delight. Elizabeth had never heard the woman say a bad word about anyone, and she was always the first to offer help when needed. She had lost her husband during the first months of the war, and both her sons were fighting overseas, yet she always had a smile and a cheerful word for everyone. It was a pleasure to buy bread and buns in her spotlessly clean and bright shop or sit in her warm, cozy parlor enjoying a spot of afternoon tea.

"I'd like to know why we are here," Deirdre demanded in her whiny voice. "I was supposed to join the Women's League knitting group this afternoon. I trust this issue is important enough to summon us in the middle of the week?"

Wally took his pipe out of his mouth and waved it at her. "Settle down, Deirdre. Her ladyship would not have called this meeting if it weren't important. Now ain't that so, your ladyship?"

"Quite so, Captain Carbunkle." Elizabeth cleared her throat. "I've called you all here because of the unpleasant hostility that prevails in the village toward the Americans. I believe the matter is serious enough that it's time to do something about it. Apparently the Tudor Arms was badly damaged last night when a fight broke out between the British soldiers and the Americans. I find this situation unacceptable, and we have to come up with ways to improve matters."

"I told you this would happen," Deirdre muttered.

Elizabeth sighed. "It's true, Mrs. Cumberland and her grievance committee discussed the matter with me a while ago, but nothing has been done about it, and the situation is simply getting worse. Does anyone have any ideas of how we can alleviate the problem?"

"Close down the aerodrome, that's what I say," Percy declared. "Bloody Yanks are causing more trouble than they are worth. Sorry, your ladyship, but I've had it up to here with them." He drew his hand across his throat.

"I think we all have to remember just why the Americans are here." Elizabeth squared her shoulders, prepared to fight if needs be. "Every day those young men risk their lives in the skies to help us win this war. Some of them die. Some of them are horribly disfigured. In my opinion, we should be going down on our knees to thank them, instead of blaming them for everything that goes wrong in the village."

"Hear, hear, m'm," Bessie murmured. "They're good lads, they are. Just a long way from home." She sent Deirdre her beautiful smile. "I hope and pray every day that if my sons end up in a strange town in a foreign country, someone will be kind enough to take care of them for me. I wouldn't mind betting there are plenty of mothers in America praying for the same thing."

Deirdre sniffed, but Wally clapped his hands. "Well said, Bessie, me old mate. So how can we help the poor blighters feel at home?"

"I was thinking we should offer some kind of entertainment that both the English and the Americans could enjoy together." Elizabeth looked around the table. "Something that will take them out of the pub every night."

"Like a concert?" Percy shook his head. "Begging your pardon, m'm, I can't see the Yanks sitting still that long. Energetic lot, they are. Always on the go. I've seen them in my shop. Can't stand still a minute, they can't. Always jiggling about, shuffling their feet like they want to dance all the time."

"That's it!" Elizabeth snapped her fingers. "We'll hold a dance for them."

The expressions on the faces of the council members didn't look encouraging. Even Bessie looked doubtful at the suggestion.

"We have the monthly dance at the village hall," Deirdre said stiffly. "I suppose we could invite them there."

Wally let out a roar of laughter. "Can you see them jazzed-up Yanks trotting around the village hall to the music of Ernie's Entertainers? What with Wilf wheezing on the mouth organ and Ernie's caterwauling on his trumpet, and poor old Priscilla Peeble playing on the cracks between the piano keys, there'd be a flipping riot before the first song came to an end."

"Not at the village hall," Elizabeth said impatiently.

"I mean here, at the town hall. We have enough space out there in the ballroom to accommodate everyone. We could decorate it ourselves, and Ted Wilkins could supply beer and wine from his pub. Maybe the Americans could bring some spirits from the base. I'm sure someone could arrange that."

Wally nodded. "You might have something there, your ladyship. But what would we do about music? Ernie would be booed off the stage."

"We could play records!" Bessie announced. "I've got a whole pile of band music—American and English. I've got nearly all of those Glen Miller tunes. My Philip collects them. We could use my gramophone, and I know Philip wouldn't mind if we used his speakers. Oo, it's going to be lovely!"

Her enthusiasm rippled around the table. "I'll be master of ceremonies," Wally offered, "and Percy here can run the gramophone."

"I suppose I could ask the Women's League to decorate," Deirdre said rather wistfully. "It might be quite enjoyable. It has been a dreadfully long time since Roland and I danced together."

"I'll make some sausage rolls and Cornish pasties." Bessie sent a sly glance at Percy. " 'Course, it would help if I could get my hands on a little of that black market stuff."

Percy nodded. "I'll see what I can do, though I can't promise, mind."

Bessie clapped her hands. "Ted can get some crisps and nuts. Oo, I can't wait."

Well pleased with herself, Elizabeth beamed at everyone. "That's settled, then. We'll do it."

"When shall we have it?" Wally asked. "I'll need to rehearse a bit."

"As soon as possible." Elizabeth took a deep breath. "This Saturday."

A chorus of dismay met her words.

"That's only two days away!"

"We can't get everything done by then!"

"That's impossible!"

This last was from Deirdre. Bessie, Elizabeth noted, said nothing, though her smile had faltered.

"Nothing is impossible if we put our minds to it." Elizabeth straightened her back. "This is a war effort to improve relationships between the allies. It has top priority over everything else. If we all work together we can get it done."

"Well," Deirdre said, "it might be an idea if Rita Crumm and her cohorts stop looking for Nazis and give us a hand. We'll need all the help we can get."

Well satisfied, Elizabeth nodded. "I intend to do just that. This dance will be just the thing to take their minds off that German pilot."

"I imagine you will be there to greet everyone at the door, Lady Elizabeth?"

"Of course I'll be there."

"You'll be bringing your American officers, then?" Wally asked, puffing furiously on his pipe. "Might be a good idea. They can keep their chaps from getting out of hand."

"Who's going to keep our lads from getting out of hand?" Percy demanded.

All four pairs of eyes turned in Elizabeth's direction. She gave them all a weak smile. Violet's words echoed in her head. All she could hope was that they were not prophetic and that she wasn't taking on more trouble than she could handle.

CHAPTER

❈ 10 ❈

When Elizabeth arrived at the Macclesby farm a few minutes later, it was to confront utter chaos. Pigs ran around loose in the yard, chased by red-faced soldiers carrying rifles, while a female voice, unmistakably belonging to Rita Crumm, could be heard from the cornfields screeching curses at the top of her lungs. George stood on the bottom rung of a gate, hollering orders that no one seemed to hear, let alone obey.

Elizabeth saw Pauline over by the cowshed, arguing with an army officer, and in the distance a group of women brandishing what she fervently hoped weren't carving knives advanced in a solid line upon the only haystack that appeared to be intact. The rest were torn apart and scattered to the winds.

As she crossed the yard to the house, the unpleasant smell of burning wool caught her attention. A thin column of smoke arose from behind the farmhouse, and she hurried back there to investigate, half afraid that Rita in her enthusiasm had set fire to the barn.

Much to her relief, the smoke drifted from a smoldering bonfire. She was about to turn away when she caught sight of something glinting in the afternoon sunshine. Sparks sprayed from the ashes when she poked them with her shoe, and she saw the sunlight glance off several small pieces of metal. After a few more nudges at them with her foot, she managed to separate them from the embers.

While she waited for them to cool down, she crouched down to examine the pieces more closely. They were round, brass buttons, embossed with some kind of emblem. She waited a moment longer, then picked up the still-warm buttons and slipped them into the pocket of her cardigan.

Frowning, she straightened. Why would Sheila burn clothes, when the village was in the middle of a huge clothing drive for the victims bombed out of their homes? There was only one way to find out, and that was to ask her.

As she rounded the house, Elizabeth caught sight of Pauline striding across the yard with a bucket in her hand. She hailed the young woman, who paused, obviously irritated by this further interruption.

"Good afternoon, m'm," she mumbled, when Elizabeth approached.

"Pauline, I was wondering about that bonfire at the back of the house," Elizabeth said, coming straight to the point. "I couldn't help noticing that some clothes had been burned. Do you know anything about that?"

Pauline's face seemed to close up. "Yes, m'm. I was the one what lit it, wasn't I. Mrs. Macclesby gave me some old sacks to burn, but there weren't no clothes on there. Not that I put there, anyhow."

Elizabeth took the buttons from her pocket and held them out on her palm. "Then how do you think these got into the fire?"

Pauline stared at the buttons for several seconds. "I don't know," she said at last. "They could have been there already when I set light to the sacks. We burn a lot of stuff on that bit of ground."

"But you didn't notice them there when you put the sacks on the ground?"

Pauline looked her straight in the eye. "No, m'm. I didn't."

Satisfied, Elizabeth nodded. "Well, thank you, Pauline. I'll let you get back to work."

"Thank you, m'm. Though I don't know what work'll get done with all these army blokes running around here. Anyone can see that German ain't here. That's the army for you, always wasting someone's time." She stomped off, leaving Elizabeth to wonder if the girl's bitterness toward the military stemmed more from the loss of her boyfriend than the unwarranted interruption of her day.

Sheila opened the door to Elizabeth's summons a minute or two later, though barely more than a crack. When she recognized her visitor, however, she widened the gap and urged Elizabeth inside. "So good of you to come, Lady Elizabeth," she said, as she slammed the door shut, "though I don't really know what you can do about all this. The P.C.s have been out there for an hour trying to get rid of everyone."

Elizabeth gave her a sympathetic smile. "Well, perhaps I can at least talk to Rita. I have some news to give her anyway."

Sheila looked concerned. "Her Bert's all right, isn't he?"

"Yes, as far as I know." Elizabeth seated herself on the couch. "Don't worry, this is good news. We are holding a dance on Saturday at the town hall. I'm hoping Rita and her group of ladies will be able to help us."

"A dance?" Sheila's face brightened just a little. "What sort of dance?"

"Well, we'll be playing records—band music, of course—and we'll have drinks and refreshments. We're inviting the British soldiers as well as the Americans."

"Taking a bit of a chance there, your ladyship. Our boys don't get on with the Yanks too well."

"That's just the point. We want to create an environment where both sides can get to know each other and appreciate each other's point of view."

Sheila still looked doubtful. "And you're sure that can happen at a dance where there's drinking and girls?"

Elizabeth felt a stab of apprehension. Now that she really thought about it, maybe it wasn't such a good idea after all. In the next instant she chided herself. She couldn't let a few niggling doubts get in the way. The die was cast now, and she would see it through to the bitter end. Never say die; that was the Hartleigh motto. Those words had given her ancestors courage and conviction through wars and battles in the past, and it would get her through whatever lay ahead.

Remembering the buttons, she pulled them from her pocket. "I found these lying near the bonfire around the back of the house," she said, holding them out for Sheila's inspection. "I was wondering if they belonged to the clothes you burned on the bonfire."

Sheila looked startled. "Clothes? I haven't burned any clothes. I gave Pauline some old sacks to burn, but there weren't any clothes. I give all our old clothes to the village clothing drive."

"Ah, that was what I wanted to mention," Elizabeth said hurriedly. "I didn't know if you were aware of the drive."

"Everyone knows about it, m'm. There are notices all over the town." Sheila glanced at the clock. "I'm so sorry, Lady Elizabeth. You've been here for ten minutes, and I haven't even offered you some tea. Would you like a cup?"

"That's very kind of you," Elizabeth said, rising to her feet, "but I think I'll get out there and talk to Rita before her ladies do any more damage to your haystacks."

"Thank you, m'm, I'd appreciate that. Nothing I say does any good. When I told them they were trespassing, Rita kept telling me it's wartime, and the rules don't count anymore. What I say is that no matter if there's a war on or not, a person's property is private, and I should be able to order them off my land."

"Quite right, Sheila. I'll see to it right away." Elizabeth turned to leave, then paused. "Before I go, though, I wonder if you'd mind taking a closer look at these buttons? They are rather distinctive, and I'd like to know if you remember seeing them anywhere before."

She held out the buttons, and Sheila took them into her hand as if afraid they would burn her skin. She turned them over, then hastily handed them back to Elizabeth. "Sorry, m'm. Never saw them before in my life. I'm sorry I can't help you."

"That's all right." Elizabeth opened the door. "Maybe one of the girls will recognize them. I hope you won't mind if I have a word with them?"

For a moment or two Sheila looked as if she might argue, but then she shook her head. "Not at all, your ladyship."

"Thank you, Sheila. I promise I'll be as quick as I can."

Elizabeth closed the door, then jumped as Sid's grating voice said behind her, "Lady Elizabeth! I thought I saw you a little while ago. Come to help us find that bloody German, have you?"

"Not exactly, Sid." Elizabeth gave him her brightest smile. "I'm sure I can leave that to you and George."

"That you can, m'm. That you can." Sid puffed out his chest and beamed all over his face.

For a moment Elizabeth was tempted to show him the buttons then thought better of it. It had already occurred to her that if clothes had indeed been burned on the bonfire, they could possibly belong to the killer and would no doubt have been stained with Amelia's blood. It was also possible the clothes had been hidden among the sacks by the killer, knowing they would soon be destroyed.

Then again, the clothes could have been discarded by the German pilot, simply to avoid being recognized, though so far no one had reported any clothes stolen, and Elizabeth doubted that the German would be running around the countryside in his underwear. In any case, even if the clothes had been evidence, they were in ashes now and therefore not much use.

As for the buttons, if she handed them over now, she would lose any chance of finding out to whom they belonged. All in all, it seemed prudent to hang on to them for the time being.

She found Maisie in the cornfield, the sleeves of her shirt rolled up to the elbows, stubbornly refusing offers from two young soldiers to help her stack sheaves. The young girl's face glowed red with exertion as she heaved a heavy load of the corn on its end.

"Cor, look at them muscles," one of the soldiers said, poking his grinning companion in the shoulder. "I'd watch it if I were you, Doug. She could pick both of us up with one hand."

"Yeah, right bruiser, this one is." The second soldier gave Maisie's shoulder a light punch. "How about a wrestling match then, darlin'? First one on the ground loses."

Maisie looked as if she were about to cry.

Elizabeth thinned her lips and marched over to them. "Young man, why aren't you with the rest of your regiment? I was under the impression you were ordered to search for an enemy soldier, not harass the young ladies."

The soldier named Doug gave her a dirty look. "So who are you then? The sergeant major's girlfriend?"

Maisie gasped and stared at the soldier in horror at this audacious affront.

Undaunted, Elizabeth drew herself up to her full

height. "I'm Lady Elizabeth Hartleigh. May I ask whom I am addressing?"

The soldier appeared taken aback.

"His name is Private Doug McDaniel," Maisie said helpfully, earning a black scowl for her efforts.

"Well, Private McDaniel," Elizabeth said grimly, "I suggest you apologize to this young lady and then get back to your duties this very minute, or I shall have no alternative but to report your boorish behavior to your commanding officer, whom, I might add, is a very good friend of mine."

The soldier's scowl changed to concern. "Sorry, m'm," he muttered, "I didn't mean no harm."

Maisie just nodded, while the soldiers backed away then turned tail and raced across the field. "Thank you, your ladyship," she said when the men had climbed over the fence and disappeared from view.

"Not at all." Elizabeth dusted her gloved hands together. "You have to be firm with these young men today, or they will take advantage of you."

Maisie's cheeks turned red again, and she looked down at her boots. "Yes, m'm. I'll try." She peeked up again. "Are you really a great friend of their commanding officer?"

"Never met him," Elizabeth said cheerfully, "but I'm not above telling a little fib or two when it's absolutely necessary."

Maisie smiled, transforming her rather plain face into something quite pleasing. "Thank you, m'm."

"Yes, well." Elizabeth cleared her throat. "Maisie, I was wondering if you could help me with something?"

"I'll try," Maisie said, apparently eager now to return the favor.

"Well, it's about the spade you left leaning against the house the night Amelia died. You found it in the tool shed the next day, is that right?"

"Yes, m'm." Maisie seemed troubled. "I didn't do nothing wrong, did I?"

"No, no, not at all." Elizabeth smiled at the girl to reassure her. "It's just that when you found the spade you seemed really surprised to see that it was clean."

"I was!" Maisie nodded with enthusiasm. "I left it all muddied up and forgot about it. We're supposed to clean the tools before we put them away. Someone must have cleaned it up for me. That was really nice of them to do that."

Something in Elizabeth's face must have alerted her, because her smile faltered, and she added hesitantly, "Why are you asking about . . . oh!" Her hand slapped her mouth over her gasp. When she took her hand away again, the color had drained from her face. "You think Amelia was killed with my spade?"

Maisie might be naive, Elizabeth thought ruefully, but she wasn't stupid. "It's a very remote possibility," she said quickly, "so I'd appreciate it if you didn't say anything to anyone about it just yet. We don't want to cause a lot of trouble over nothing."

Maisie looked scared, but she nodded. "Mum's the word," she said, holding up her right hand. "On my honor."

"I'm most grateful. By the way, where exactly did you leave the spade that night?"

Maisie thought about it. "Standing against the wall right under Mrs. Macclesby's bedroom window," she said at last.

"Thank you, Maisie. You've been a big help. Oh, before I forget . . ." Elizabeth reached in her pocket and pulled out the buttons. "Have you ever seen these buttons before?"

Maisie peered at them. "Well, I couldn't be sure about it, of course. Some of those buttons look all the same. But . . ." She paused, as if reluctant to finish the sentence.

"Yes?" Elizabeth prompted.

"Well, as I said, I couldn't be sure of course, but they look like the buttons on a reefer jacket. Maurice wears one all the time, and his has got buttons like that."

Elizabeth closed her fingers over the buttons. "Thank you, Maisie. I won't keep you any longer. I hope you won't mention this to anyone else."

"No, m'm. You can count on me. Cross me heart and hope to die." She drew a cross with her thumb over her chest.

Elizabeth had to leave it at that.

As she hurried across the field to where Rita Crumm's army of housewives were ravaging the haystack, she couldn't help wondering if she'd been wrong about Maurice. In spite of his gentle nature, she had to remember that everyone is capable of murder if given enough reason.

If Amelia Brunswick had cruelly rejected him one time too many, it was entirely possible that something had snapped in Maurice's unstable mind, and in a fit of rage he hit her with the spade, without even understanding the consequences of his action.

It was also possible, she reminded herself, that Sheila knew what he had done and was covering for him. Which would explain her determination to point her finger at the German pilot. She could hardly blame the woman. After all, it was a mother's natural and fierce instinct to protect her young.

She reached the group of women just as Rita yelled from behind the haystack, "That's it, ladies, he's not here. Reform and regroup!"

The bedraggled women climbed wearily out of the demolished haystack and stood in a huddle, awaiting further orders. They seemed relieved to see Elizabeth and called out a chorus of greetings, no doubt alerting Rita to her presence.

Elizabeth waited for her to make an appearance. It was worth the wait.

Rita marched into view, her hat askew over one eye and a large piece of straw sticking out of her frizzy curls. Pieces of hay clung to her heavily padded shoulders and her pencil thin skirt. Ladders ran up and down her thick lisle stockings, and a metal buckle was missing from one of her shoes.

Apparently unaware of the spectacle she made, she looked haughtily down her nose at Elizabeth. "Your ladyship. Is there something we can do for you?"

"As a matter of fact, there is." Elizabeth glanced around the subdued group of women. "But this isn't the place to discuss it. You all look incredibly weary. Why don't we all meet in Bessie's tearoom in about an hour? We can discuss the matter over afternoon tea."

Rita folded her arms. "We are on an important mission, Lady Elizabeth. I'm sure the ladies would rather you tell us what you want from us right here, so that we can go on looking for that miserable Nazi."

"Did I mention you are all invited as my guests?"

The reaction from the group was immediate and emphatic. "I'll be there!" someone called out.

"Me, too!"

"I'm coming as well!"

Obviously realizing she was vastly outnumbered, Rita drew herself up to attention—a move that was spoiled somewhat when the piece of straw in her hair dislodged itself and slid down her nose. Swiping at it with her hand, she said stiffly, "Very well, if you insist. In one hour, then."

Clara Rigglesby, one of the few of Rita's followers bold enough to challenge her, spoke up. "You'd better make sure you clean up first, Rita. You look like a bloody scarecrow."

A couple of the women giggled.

"We all look like we've had a romp in the hay with the army boys," someone else said.

"Wish we had," a young woman declared. "It might have been worth all this blinking effort."

A chorus of laughter greeted this remark.

Elizabeth recognized Nellie Smith and smiled. Everyone knew Nellie was still looking for a husband and was fast approaching the age when she'd be considered an old maid.

Rita must have sensed she was losing control, for she lifted her chin and snapped, "I'll thank you all to remember that we have the lady of the manor in our presence. So forget the vulgar remarks and prepare to return to the village."

A general muttering of resentment followed her command, but the women slowly dispersed and headed for the gate.

"I hope whatever you have in mind doesn't take too long, Lady Elizabeth," Rita said as she accompanied Elizabeth back to the farmyard. "We must find this murderer and make sure he's punished for what he did to that poor girl. We can't allow anything to stop us from carrying out our duty."

"I quite understand your concern, Rita," Elizabeth assured her. She reached the gate and waited for the other woman to open it for her. "I can promise you, however, that my proposal is quite important to the war effort, and I feel confident that you and your band of followers are the best people to undertake this assignment."

In spite of her efforts to appear indifferent, Rita began to look quite excited. "Well, then, I shall look forward to hearing about this mission at the tearoom," she said as she climbed onto her bicycle.

Elizabeth lifted her hand. "In one hour, Rita." She watched the line of housewives wobble off along the lane then made her way to the cowshed. A group of soldiers sat around on the grass outside, apparently waiting for further orders. Elizabeth hoped for Sheila's sake that they soon received a command to move on and leave the poor woman in peace.

Before going in search of Maurice, she made her way around the farmhouse to where the bedroom windows overlooked the paddocks. A thorough examination of the ground revealed nothing. If there had been any bloodstains there, no doubt they would have been washed out by the recent rains.

She found Maurice inside the cowshed, where he was filling the bins with a mixture of shredded mangold, chaff, sugarbeet pulp, and crushed linseed cake, ready for the afternoon milking.

Elizabeth watched him in silence for a while. When he seemed more comfortable with her presence, she said quietly, "Maurice, do you know who burned the clothes on the bonfire this morning?"

Maurice went on shoveling the cow feed into the bins without any indication he'd understood.

Elizabeth tried again. "Maurice, I found some buttons. Would you look at them and tell me if you recognize them?"

Again Maurice ignored her.

Elizabeth stepped closer to the young man. "I'm sorry to bother you, Maurice, but sooner or later the constables are going to find out what happened to Amelia." She had no real confidence in that, but one could always live in hope. "It would make everything so much easier if you would tell me what really happened."

"He doesn't know what happened," a sharp voice said from behind her.

Elizabeth swung around to face Sheila Macclesby. She felt a nervous tug in her stomach when she saw the irate expression on Sheila's face. Obviously she'd overstepped the mark this time and now had some explaining to do.

CHAPTER

❈ 11 ❈

"Excuse me, Lady Elizabeth, but I thought I told you that Maurice doesn't know anything about what happened to Amelia."

Sheila's voice shook with barely concealed anger, and Elizabeth held up her hands in apology.

"You did, Sheila, and I'm sorry. But I just thought I'd show Maurice the buttons to see if he recognized them."

Sheila held out her hand, which trembled visibly. "Please give them to me, and I'll ask him myself."

Elizabeth emptied the buttons into the woman's hand and watched her walk over to her son.

In a completely different tone of voice Sheila said quietly, "Maurice, tell me if you've seen these buttons before."

Maurice went on shoveling feed into the bins.

"Maurice," Sheila repeated. "You must tell us if you've seen these buttons before. I need to know now. No one's going to hurt you, Maurice. You know I won't allow that."

Very slowly, Maurice turned his head and looked at his mother's face, then at the buttons in her hand.

"Have you seen them, Maurice?"

The boy moved his head from side to side in a negative shake.

"Good boy. Now go on with what you're doing." Sheila patted him on the shoulder then turned back to Elizabeth. "You'll have to excuse him, m'm. It's the shock, you see. He hasn't spoken since the night Amelia died."

She'd barely finished speaking when the most terrible sound echoed through the rafters of the cowshed.

Elizabeth's stomach turned when she realized the awful noise was coming from Maurice—his head thrown back as the agonized wail poured from his mouth in a torrent of uncontrolled grief.

"Oh, poor baby!" Sheila cried and rushed over to his side, her arms enfolding him against her bosom.

Elizabeth left them there, certain she would never forget that dreadful sound for as long as she lived. She was almost at the door of the shed when she saw a navy blue jacket hanging from a nail on one of the doorposts. It was a reefer jacket, and as far as she could see, every highly polished button was intact.

An hour later she parked her motorcycle in the street alongside the tearoom and prepared herself for the forthcoming ordeal. Once Rita found out that the important mission was nothing more demanding than decorating the town hall for a dance, Elizabeth was quite certain she would raise all kinds of objections.

It was up to her, Elizabeth reminded herself, to make the assignment sound as exciting as possible. In any case, it would do some of these women good to get involved with something frivolous for a change. The war had made things so unutterably dreary, it was up to all of them to make an effort to enjoy themselves for once.

The tearoom was once a part of a rather impressive house, owned by a wealthy merchant at the turn of the century. Shortly after Elizabeth was born, the merchant fell upon bad times, due mostly to the collapse of the British Empire. Deprived of most of his foreign trade, the merchant auctioned his house and moved to London in pursuit of more lucrative endeavors.

Bessie's father had won the bid and turned the servants' quarters into a bakery. The wall between the once elegant drawing room and the vast library had been torn down and the space converted into a fashionable tearoom. Bessie, as sole heir, had inherited the business upon her father's death.

Having been taught as a child and handed down her father's secret recipes, Bessie proved to be an even better pastry chef than he had been. She had added her own special touches to the quaint tearoom, such as hand-painted flower boxes on all the window sills, shiny horse brasses pinned to black and red leather straps hanging on the walls, and bright copper tea urns decorating the fireplace, where a coal fire burned for much of the year.

Delicate lace curtains hung at the leaded pane windows, and embroidered lace edged the white linen tablecloths, which were lovingly laundered by Bessie and hung on the line to dry in the back garden. The fragrance of fresh flowers and greenery wafted around the arrangements on each table, mingling with the delightful aroma of coffee and fresh-baked bread.

The room had an aura of welcome about it, as if one were paying a private visit to a dear friend's house, and the cheerful service given by Bessie's staff emphasized that feeling. Although Elizabeth rarely visited the tearoom, she invariably enjoyed herself here and came away with a conviction that, like the Manor House, as long as Bessie's tearoom was there, the traditions of Sitting Marsh would remain relatively unscathed by the ravages of war.

The clamor of chattering voices faded one by one when Elizabeth stepped through the door, until a respectful hush fell over the room. Rita rose from her seat at the table nearest the door, where no doubt she had been holding court over the entire room.

"Lady Elizabeth," she announced in the haughty tone she reserved for such an occasion.

Elizabeth graciously inclined her head at the murmured echoes of greetings. "I do hope I haven't kept you all waiting."

"Not at all, your ladyship," Rita said briskly. "I think everyone is here. I have reserved a chair for you at my table."

Elizabeth stifled her pang of resentment at Rita's obvious attempt to upstage her. "Thank you, Rita, that is most kind of you." She took the seat offered her and sat down, smoothing her skirt beneath her.

Bessie came bustling out, her face wreathed in smiles as usual. "Lady Elizabeth! I thought I heard your voice. The ladies informed me you were hosting this event this afternoon."

Elizabeth smiled back. "That's right, Bessie. Please bring everyone afternoon tea, and I'll settle with you later." She would have to come up with a brilliant plan for the settlement of such a large bill, she thought as Bessie scurried away to the kitchen. But that could wait until later. Her proposition was the important issue at that moment.

"Ladies! I have an announcement to make," she called out, rising to her feet again. "I'd like to get the business part of this meeting over with first, then we can all relax and enjoy our tea."

An array of hats with curious eyes beneath the various brims turned in her direction.

She waited until she had everyone's rapt attention then cleared her throat. "As you are no doubt aware, relations between the Americans and the people of Sitting Marsh have been somewhat strained. I would like to attempt to remedy that."

A smattering of comments greeted her words, while Rita began, "If I might—"

Elizabeth silenced them all with a raised hand. "Please hear me out, then everyone can have their say. I called a council meeting this afternoon, and we have decided to hold a dance in honor of our American guests. Everyone will be invited, including the soldiers from Beerstowe."

This time the chatter was much more vibrant. Elizabeth had to shout in order to be heard. "Ladies! The dance will be held this Saturday, and since this is such short notice, we desperately need your help to decorate the town hall and perhaps help Bessie provide refreshments."

Again a burst of comments and questions broke forth. Rita's cheeks glowed as she rose, one hand raised to silence her followers. "Ladies, please." She turned to Elizabeth. "A dance at the town hall, your ladyship? In two days? Isn't that asking just a bit too much?"

"Go on, Rita, you're just jealous you didn't think of it first." Clara Rigglesby smirked as the others giggled.

"You're right," someone else said. "Blimey, just think of the fun we could have at a dance with them Yanks."

"Better hope our husbands don't get to hear of it, then," muttered Joan Plumstone, a thin-faced woman with a sour disposition.

"Oh, belt up, Joan," her companion said, giving her a nudge in the arm. "Who's going to tell them? What the eyes don't see the heart won't grieve over."

"Yeah, don't forget. Loose lips sink ships."

Nellie Smith, now wearing a large, floppy-brimmed hat, waved her hand. "Your ladyship, does that mean you're inviting the soldiers from the camp as well?"

"Anyone who wants to come," Elizabeth assured her.

"How much is it going to cost to go, m'm?" Clara asked.

"I hadn't really thought about that." Elizabeth did some fast calculations in her head. "I suppose we could charge everyone sixpence, the way we do at the village hall."

"At least a shilling," Rita argued, apparently realizing she was outnumbered in her skepticism. "After all, the town hall is much bigger and better than the village hall."

"We're not going to have Ernie's Entertainers, are we?" someone asked.

A chorus of deep groans followed that question.

"No, we're not." Bessie arrived on the scene carrying a huge tray loaded with teapots. "We're going to play my Philip's records. You'd all better learn to jive and jitterbug if you're going to dance with the Yanks."

A ripple of excitement ran through the crowd.

"I'd like to see a Yank throw me over his shoulder," a chubby woman commented.

"Better make sure you're wearing your knickers, Margie," someone else commented.

An eager-looking woman seated by the window raised her hand. "What about the land girls, m'm? Will they be coming?"

"They'll be invited," Elizabeth assured Florrie Evans.

"Ooh, 'eck," someone muttered, "we'll have to fight them off if we want to dance with the Yanks."

Everyone started talking at once, and Elizabeth clapped her hands. She clapped them twice more and begged for silence, still without success.

Deciding to take matters into her own hands, Rita stepped forward and bellowed, "Bleeding well shut your mouths, will you! Her ladyship's trying to speak!"

Momentarily deafened, Elizabeth clasped her throat as the room fell silent once more. "I just want to remind everyone," she said after a pause to collect her thoughts, "that this dance is an effort to restore harmony between the Americans and the people of Sitting Marsh. There will be British soldiers at the dance, just as eager and just as capable of dancing with you as the Americans. I trust you will all remember that and accord everyone the same courtesy. I hope those of you with daughters who might attend will impress upon them the importance of treating the British and the American military alike."

"You can impress upon them all you like," Joan muttered, "but that doesn't mean they're going to listen."

"Well, you must make them listen." Elizabeth gestured at Rita. "Now, Mrs. Crumm will take over and delegate the work of decorating the hall. I realize we have limited supplies, but wc should bc able to come up with some ideas to make the place look festive."

The discussion that followed was boisterous, loud, and none too productive. In fact, some of the suggestions were downright ludicrous. Elizabeth was quite thankful when one suggestion to use toilet rolls for decoration was shot down for lack of coupons. She did her best to ignore the uproar and concentrated on enjoying her egg and cress sandwich. The hot buttered scone that followed, lavished with Devon cream and strawberry jam, was even more delicious, especially when washed down with a cup of hot, strong tea.

Rita finally secured a list of names of those willing to meet at the town hall that evening and with an air of bravado informed Elizabeth she had nothing to worry about. "We'll do the place up, one way or another," she said, her voice lacking conviction.

"I'm sure I can rely on you and your ladies." Elizabeth rose from the table. "If there's anything I can do to help, please don't hesitate to ask. I'll have Polly hunt for something that might be useful. My parents used to decorate the Manor House for special occasions. There might be something in the attics you could use."

"Thank you, your ladyship, but we don't want to posh it up too much, do we," Rita said, her expression smug. "After all, this won't exactly be the society ball of the year. We don't want the ordinary people to feel out of place."

"Perhaps not," Elizabeth said quietly. "On the other hand, we don't want it to look like Saturday night at the boozer, either." She moved to the door. "Of course, one has to know the difference. I'll send Violet down to supervise. I think a certain amount of taste would not be amiss." Well pleased with the look of outrage on Rita's face, she closed the door firmly behind her and headed for the bake shop.

Bessie was behind the counter, discussing with the three ladies who worked for her the items to be baked for the dance. She smiled at Elizabeth as she walked in. "There you are, your ladyship. I was just telling my girls we'll have to bake all night to get everything done. But it will be worth it, won't it, ladies?"

Elsie, Helen, and Janet nodded in enthusiastic agreement.

"Thank you all," Elizabeth said warmly. "I'm sorry it's such short notice, but I think the situation warrants a certain amount of haste. I'm hoping we can all set an example for the military and prove that we can all get along quite well together if we put our minds to it."

"I hope you're right, m'm," Bessie murmured, echoing Elizabeth's lingering doubts. "But we'll give it a jolly good try, anyway."

"Yes, well," Elizabeth rubbed at a nonexistent spot on the counter, "about the funds for all this. I—"

"Don't you worry about nothing, m'm," Bessie assured her. "If they all pay a shilling to get in, that should be enough to cover everything, including this afternoon's tea meeting. There's always the war effort fund if we're a bit short. After all, this is a war effort, isn't it?"

Elizabeth sighed. "Thank you, Bessie. I just hope we're doing the right thing."

"Of course we are." Bessie turned to her helpers.

"Well, get on with it. You'd better get cracking if you want to get some sleep tonight."

The women scurried into the kitchen, and Bessie leaned her plump, dimpled elbows on the counter. "I know it's none of my business, your ladyship, but I was wondering if they found out who killed that poor land girl yet."

"Not as far as I know," Elizabeth admitted.

"Seems like that German killed her, then?"

"I really don't know what to think," Elizabeth said carefully. "So far no one seems to know with whom Amelia spent that last evening. He or she might have been able to answer some important questions."

"Well, maybe I can help you there." Bessie looked over her shoulder at the door to the kitchen, which was firmly closed. "I wasn't sure if I should tell you this, but I just found out a little while ago that Elsie's brother, Tim, is stationed out at the camp in Beerstowe. He saw a young woman creeping out of the sick bay just before midnight the night the land girl was killed. The only patient in there at the time was a friend of Tim's. His name is Jeff Thomas, and he'd been going out with the girl who was killed. Tim's pretty sure it was her he saw creeping out of there that night. He didn't say anything to the police because he didn't want to get Jeff in trouble. Especially now his girlfriend is dead. But I thought you might want to know."

"I see," Elizabeth said slowly. "Thank you, Bessie, for letting me know."

She left the shop, mulling over this latest piece of information. Amelia apparently did spend the evening with Jeff Thomas after all and had left there alive, presumably to come home alone. Sheila Macclesby heard the girl arguing with someone after she arrived back at the farm. The German pilot? Or Maurice? It certainly seemed that the suspects had been narrowed down to those two, and although Elizabeth hated to admit it, it was beginning to look more and more as though one of them had taken a spade to Amelia's head.

She went over the possible scenarios in her head as she rode her motorcycle back to the Manor House. The remaining land girls were still a possibility, of course, but only one of them had any real motive, and although Pauline's attitude wasn't the most pleasant she'd come across, Elizabeth couldn't picture her wielding a spade at a young woman's head. Then again, none of her suspects seemed capable of such a ghastly attack.

There was always the possibility that the German pilot had been discovered lurking in the yard when Amelia arrived home that night. Perhaps he'd panicked, killed the girl to silence her, then taken her body to the woods to secure his hiding place. Had he then exchanged his blood-stained uniform for clothes stolen from the farmhouse and hidden them in the sacks to be burned?

Or had Maurice killed Amelia in a fit of rage? Perhaps Sheila had found his bloodstained clothes and burned them to protect him.

Whatever had really happened, it seemed unlikely anyone would be able to prove anything. Unless she could trace the origin of the buttons she'd found.

She would pay a visit to Rosie Finnegan the very next day, she decided. Rosie owned the clothes shop in the High Street. Maybe she could help find out to what garment those buttons were attached. If they didn't come from Maurice's reefer jacket, then perhaps they came from the German pilot's uniform. It wasn't much, but right then it was all she had. And something told her she had to get at the truth soon, before an innocent person was convicted of murder.

CHAPTER

❧ 12 ❧

"Did you hear about the dance on Saturday?" Marlene asked eagerly the minute Polly put her foot inside the door that night.

Still flushed from the kiss Sam gave her before he dropped her off at the house, Polly had to collect her thoughts a bit before she answered. "Dance? What dance?"

Marlene waltzed down the narrow hallway to the kitchen, her red hair swinging above her shoulders. "Her ladyship is putting on a dance at the town hall and guess what!"

Polly followed her, intrigued by her older sister's excitement. "Clark Gable is coming."

"Not bloomin' likely, silly." Marlene pushed open the kitchen door and disappeared inside.

Polly hung her coat up on the hallstand and rushed into the kitchen behind her. "So tell me what!"

Marlene grabbed her startled mother and swung her
around, spraying water from the potato peeler she held
in her hand. "Go on, Ma, tell Polly about the dance!"

Edna Barnett sighed. "Rita and the rest of us all had
tea with Lady Elizabeth this afternoon, and—"

"What?" Polly gaped at her in astonishment. "What,
up at the Manor House? I didn't see none of you up
there."

"Not at the Manor House," Edna explained patiently.
"At Bessie's tearoom. Her ladyship paid for everything."

"Why'd she do that?"

"Because she wanted to ask us if we'd help decorate
the town hall tonight. The council is putting on a dance
on Saturday night."

"Ah," Polly murmured, nodding her head, "so that's
why she had me pull out all that stuff from the store-
rooms. I thought she was going to spruce up the Manor
House a bit."

Marlene gave her mother a hefty nudge. "Go on, tell
her who's invited."

"You already told me it weren't Clark Gable." Polly
flopped down on the nearest chair. "I'm not much in-
terested in anyone else."

"What about if we told you that the soldiers from
Beerstowe have been invited, as well as all the Yanks?"

Polly frowned. "The Yanks won't come. They came
that once to the village hall dance, remember? They
stayed long enough to eat up all the sandwiches, then
they left and went down the pub. Never danced one
dance, they didn't. Just stood around looking like a
bunch of strays caught in a storm."

Marlene bounced onto the chair next to her. "They
didn't stay because no one can dance to Awful Ernie's
music. But what if they had real American big band
music that they could jive to and jitterbug? They'd
bloody well come then, wouldn't they?"

"Watch your language, Marlene," Edna warned, still
busily peeling potatoes.

"Sorry, Ma." Marlene leaned forward and dug her nail into Polly's arm. "You could ask your Sam to come. He'd bring his mates, wouldn't he?"

Polly felt a shiver of excitement. "He might. I could ask him." Her smile faded. "Too bad about Clay. You could have asked him, too."

Marlene's face sobered, too. "I know. Poor bugger. I keep thinking about him, wondering what happened to him."

"Probably picked up by the Germans now," Polly said, feeling sorry for her sister.

Marlene nodded. "Well, that's war, I suppose. At least he won't have to fly those planes again. Not like Sam. You must feel ill every time he goes up in them."

Polly shrugged. "I do, but what's the use of worrying? If it's his time, then there's nothing anyone can do about it." Her words hid the cold dread she felt every time she thought about Sam taking off with a load of bombs sitting underneath him. He'd been lucky so far. He'd come back in one piece. She refused to think about the unwritten law that said the more times he went up, the more likely his number would eventually be up.

Thinking about Sam reminded her of something. "Well, I've got big news meself tonight," she announced.

Edna spun around with a look of alarm on her face. "I hope it's good news," she said, shaking her potato peeler at Polly. "I hope you've been behaving yourself."

Polly snorted. " 'Course I have. Haven't had much chance to do anything else."

"And you'd better not do anything else, or your father will hear of it."

"Aw, Ma, would you shut up nagging at me." Polly leaned back in her chair. "You should be proud of me for what I done."

Edna immediately looked suspicious, while Marlene's eyes lit up. "Go on, what did you do, then?"

"I got hired to be Lady Elizabeth's secretary, that's

what," Polly proudly declared. "So what do you think of that, then?"

"You never did!" Marlene slapped her palm down on the table, making Polly jump. "I don't believe it."

"Is this true, Polly?" Edna demanded. She looked pleased in spite of the doubt in her voice.

" 'Course it's true." Polly hooked her thumbs into her hair and pulled it back from her face. "Now I'll have to put my hair up proper all the time."

"Are you getting paid more money?"

Polly pulled a face at Marlene. "Not yet, but I will when I learn everything."

"When did this happen?" Edna asked, still sounding suspicious.

"This morning." Polly sat up straight again. "I asked Lady Elizabeth if I could help out in the office, and she said yes."

"Instead of cleaning the house?"

"No, I've still got to clean, but at least I'll be doing secretary's work some of the time."

Marlene grinned. "You must really like that Sam."

"Just who *is* this Sam?" Edna demanded.

Polly scowled at her sister. "The American officer who gives me a lift home at night. He's staying at the Manor House, and he's a friend of Lady Elizabeth's."

Edna's eyes narrowed. "Just how old is this Sam?"

"Aw, Ma, I don't know, do I. He's just someone her ladyship asked to give me a lift 'cause she's worried about me riding me bike past the woods at night."

"Doesn't sound so innocent to me. How long has this been going on? What about your bike?"

"Just last night and tonight. He puts me bike in the back of the Jeep so I have it for the mornings. It's all right, Ma. Sam's a proper gentleman. He wouldn't do nothing, honest." Polly crossed her fingers under the table. Maybe it wasn't exactly the truth, but she was scared to death her mother would forbid her to see Sam again if she knew just how much her youngest daughter cared about the handsome officer.

"Well, just make sure there's no hanky-panky going on between you," Edna muttered, turning back to the sink. She lifted the pot of potatoes and dumped it on the stove. "Are you two girls going to help us decorate tonight? I think most of Rita's group is helping out."

"I've got to wash some clothes," Marlene said, getting up from the table. "I want to hang them out on the line tonight now that it's stopped raining."

"Me, too," Polly said, getting excited again about jitterbugging with Sam. "I wonder if I can talk Sam into getting us some nylons for the dance?"

Marlene grinned. "Play your cards right, me girl, and you can talk him into anything you want."

"Here!" Edna said sharply. "I don't want none of that talk in this house."

"Oh, go on, Ma, you worry too much." Marlene slapped her mother playfully on the back as she went past her. "I'm going to sort out some clothes before supper."

Polly sprang to her feet. "Me, too. I have to decide what I'm going to wear on Saturday."

"Just don't bring trouble home to this house," Edna muttered. "Neither of you. Or I'll wash my hands of you."

Polly knew what she meant. She'd heard it all before. "We won't, Ma," she promised automatically and followed Marlene upstairs to pick out her dress for the dance.

Alone in the library, Elizabeth surveyed the mound of garlands and silk flowers that had decorated the Manor House for longer than she remembered. There was far too much for her to carry on her motorcycle. She smiled when the solution occurred to her.

She had to visit the east wing in order to issue the invitation to the dance. She had already called the Amer-

ican base and the camp in Beerstowe to inform them of
the event, but she wanted to invite the major and his
officers personally. That way she could be fairly certain
that they would feel under some obligation to attend. If
the major happened to be in the east wing when she went
up there, she could ask him to help her take the decorations over to the town hall.

And if not, she reminded herself as she hurried down
the great hall, she could always ask that nice Sam Cutter,
who had been kind enough to give Polly a ride home
these past two nights.   Having convinced herself that
she was not simply making up excuses to see the major
again, she felt quite pleased with the way things were
working out.

She was halfway down the hall when she thought she
saw something moving at the far end. The double sum-
mertime provided daylight hours until quite late, and the
sun was just beginning to sink in the evening sky. The
long shadows cast from the two suits of armor stretched
from wall to wall, and it was in those shadows that Elizabeth thought she saw movement.

Even as she paused there, beneath the portrait of the
first Lord Hartleigh and his wife, she felt a strong, cold
draft of wind brush her face. Startled, she stepped back,
her fingers jumping to her cheek. None of the windows
opened along this stretch of the hall, and the doors at
both ends were securely fastened. Yet there was an unmistakable draft blowing from somewhere.

The shadows moved again, and what appeared to be
a faint mist seemed to blow across them. It hovered there
for no more than a second or two, then vanished.

Elizabeth blinked. It had all happened so fast she was
certain now that she must have imagined it. All this talk
of ghosts had unsettled her nerves. There were no such
things as ghosts. Or even if there were, surely they
waited until nightfall to make an appearance. She really
had to stop listening to Martin's ramblings.

In spite of her convictions, she trod warily down the

length of the hall until she reached the door that led to the east wing. As she stretched out her hand, a terrible gargling noise, followed by a shuddering and rattling, almost shot her out of her skin. Without another second's delay she hauled open the door and fled through it.

Her common sense told her that it was just the water pipes complaining because someone had used the lavatory. Her shattered nerves, however, propelled her forward at full steam. Head down, she charged around the corner and ran smack into a sturdy body.

Temporarily winded, she heard a startled "Ouf!" as her unfortunate companion lost the air from his lungs. She didn't have to look up to know she'd charged straight into Earl Monroe's stomach.

"I say," she muttered, "I'm terribly sorry. I'm afraid I wasn't looking where I was going. Are you all right?"

She was afraid to look at him. For one thing she was standing much too close to him. Close enough to smell a quite unusual fragrance. Very pleasant. Had to be American. British men didn't smell nearly that good. Not the ones she'd been anywhere close to, that was.

Something else she noticed, which didn't help to calm her nerves one bit, was that she was held in a quite firm grip. He'd grabbed her arms to steady her when she'd barreled into him. He hadn't let go. She could feel his fingers right through the sleeves of her silk blouse. For several seconds she remained motionless, while her heart pounded.

"We could use you on our football team," he said at last, mercifully removing his hands from her tingling arms. "You pack a real wallop, ma'am."

"Sorry," she mumbled. "Something startled me." She smoothed her fingers down her skirt, even though there were no wrinkles to be seen.

"Wouldn't happen to be the belching in those water pipes, now would it?"

She risked a guilty glance at him. Although she was

prepared for her reaction, her stomach still managed to complete a somersault. What on earth was it about the man that reduced her insides to limp spaghetti every time she looked at him? "I'm sorry. They do make a ghastly noise, I'm afraid."

"So where's the fire?"

Confused, she said uncertainly, "I beg your pardon?"

"Where were you going in such a hurry?"

"Oh!" She hesitated, reluctant to tell him she was actually looking for him. She didn't want to give him the idea that she was in that great a hurry to find him. "Actually," she said slowly, "I was coming to offer your officers an invitation."

His quizzical look was almost comical. "You're going to invite them all to dinner?"

"No, to dance," she said hurriedly.

"You want to dance with my officers?"

No, just one of them. She'd almost said the words out loud. "Not to dance, Major. To *a* dance. Saturday at the town hall. Actually I want to invite everyone on the base. Those who have passes, of course."

His eyebrows raised. "You want to take on the entire outfit?"

"Well, not me personally." She had the feeling he was making fun of her. Raising her chin, she said firmly, "We're inviting the soldiers from Beerstowe as well. And the land army. Of course, most of the villagers will probably be there."

"Sort of 'meet the forces' day in Sitting Marsh."

"If you like. We are concerned about the brawling that goes on between the British army and the Americans. I'm afraid the villagers haven't helped with their somewhat biased attitudes. We thought it might be a good idea to get everyone together in a social atmosphere so they can get to know each other a little better."

"Hmmm." He rubbed his chin. "Well, I guess we could give it a try, though I have to tell you, Lady Elizabeth, unless you hide the beer and liquor you could end up with a heck of a battle on your hands. Those boys need to let off steam, and that's one sure way of doing it."

"Oh, dear." Elizabeth's hand rose to her throat. "Well, I suppose we'll have to take that chance. Which is why I was hoping you'd be able to attend. Sort of keep an eye on things, as it were."

Major Monroe's mouth twitched into a smile. "Is that the only reason you're inviting me, Lady Elizabeth?"

"Well . . . no, I mean . . . of course, I'd be delighted . . . er . . . I'd appreciate it very much if you could come."

He nodded, his sharp gaze never leaving her face. "I'll come on condition that you promise me a dance."

If she'd been flustered before, it was nothing compared to her confusion now. Her hand gripped her throat until she was in dire danger of choking, while she struggled to regain her composure. When she deemed it safe to speak again, she said carefully, "I'd be delighted, Major."

He inclined his head in a slight bow. "My pleasure. I'd be real happy, ma'am, if you'd allow me to escort you there in my Jeep."

"Oh! Well, that would be very nice. Thank you." She made a mental note to be sure and tie a scarf around her hair. "Shall we meet around eight in the library?"

"Eight it is."

She couldn't seem to stop smiling at him. Feeling quite foolish, she cleared her throat loudly. "Yes, well, that's settled then. I'll leave it up to you to invite the other officers. The more we have, the more likely we can keep everything under control."

"The good Lord willing."

He'd put so much fervor into that muttered phrase she had cause for alarm again. All she could hope was that they were not all making a terrible mistake. She was about to bid him good night when she remembered her other reason for seeking him out. "I do have one more small favor to ask," she said, smiling up at him. "I have a rather large pile of decorations that I need to take down to the town hall. I was wondering if you might spare a few minutes and give me a lift down there in your Jeep. There are too many to pile into the sidecar on my motorcycle."

The major glanced at his watch. "As a matter of fact, I was just leaving for the base. I can drop you off on the way."

"Splendid! I'll meet you by the front steps, then. It won't take more than a minute or two to pick up the box."

"I have a better idea. I'll come with you and get the box so you won't have to carry it."

"That's terribly gallant of you, Major. Thank you."

"My pleasure, ma'am."

She hurried to keep up with his long stride as they headed down the great hall to the main stairs. As they passed the suits of armor, she peered at them rather hard but couldn't see anything unusual about them. *It all must have been a trick of the light just then*, she assured herself.

"I'll round up a few bottles of Scotch for the dance if you like," Monroe offered as they descended the staircase together.

Vastly relieved she hadn't had to ask him after all, she exclaimed, "Oh, would you? That would be marvelous. We'll pay you for them, of course, out of the proceeds."

He nodded. "How will you get back from the town hall?"

"Pardon?" She sent him a startled glance. That thought hadn't even occurred to her. Where was her mind wandering to lately?

"Well, you can't walk all that way back. Especially at night with a murderer on the loose." He looked sideways at her. "I guess they haven't found the German yet?"

"No, they haven't. Apparently he'd been hiding out at the Macclesby's farm, but by the time the soldiers got there, he was long gone. I was talking to the army captain on the phone just now, and he thinks the German has probably left the area. I think they are calling off the search and leaving it to the police to handle."

"Well, England is a pretty small country. There can't be too many Germans wandering around. He'll be picked up sooner or later."

"I suppose so. It does leave things sort of up in the air, though, doesn't it?" Elizabeth paused at the library door. "I suppose we shall never know now who killed poor Amelia Brunswick."

The voice came from nowhere, startling them both. "What are you doing! Halt there, I say!"

The quavery command had come from behind them, and both of them swung around.

Looking a little like a giant ant in his black morning coat, Martin advanced upon them at the speed of a tortoise, brandishing what appeared to be the blunderbuss from her father's collection of antique guns.

"What the devil—!" Earl Monroe immediately stepped in front of Elizabeth, shielding her from Martin's sight.

Terribly gratified by this show of heroism, Elizabeth basked for a moment in the unfamiliar glow of feeling thoroughly cherished and protected. It had been a long time since anyone had acted so chivalrously toward her.

Major Monroe's back was quite broad and hid Martin from view. His voice, however, could be heard quite plainly. "Unhand that lady this instant, sir, or I shall be forced to put a cannonball into your intestines."

Elizabeth winced and stepped out from behind Earl Monroe's comforting frame. "It's all right, Major," she assured him. "It isn't loaded." She took a step forward into Martin's path and held out her hand. "Give me the gun, Martin. As you can see, I'm in no danger. Major Monroe is our guest."

Martin peered over the top of his glasses. "I beg your pardon, madam, but I believe you've been misled. This is the German officer everyone is looking for. You can see his uniform is most certainly not British." He raised the gun and jabbed it in the major's direction. "Have at you, sir!"

"Are you quite sure it's not loaded?" Earl Monroe asked with just a trace of uncertainty in his voice.

"Quite," Elizabeth said confidently. "Even if it were it probably wouldn't fire. It hasn't been fired for centur—" Her words ended in a piercing scream as a deafening roar rattled the chandelier above her head.

At the same time a cloud of smoke billowed from the end of the gun, and Martin was lifted off his feet. Elizabeth just had time to see him land with a thud on his back when something hit her hard between the shoulder blades. The force of the weight behind her thrust her face down onto the carpet.

Momentarily stunned, she realized the heavy weight was still on top of her, pinning her down. Part of her mind registered the dust rising from the carpet under her nose, and she made a mental note to remind Polly to vacuum the carpet first thing in the morning.

Her mind cleared an instant later, and she realized she was in danger of expiring from lack of breath, since her lungs were crushed by the mysterious weight on her back. She heard a faint groan further down the hall then a pattering of feet running toward them.

Violet's voice sounded incredulous when she exclaimed, "What in the world are you all doing on the floor?"

The weight on her back shifted, and Elizabeth raised her head. A few feet away, Martin lay on his back, the gun still in his grip and pointing straight at the ceiling.

"You okay?"

The major's voice spoke directly in her ear, and she realized it was his body lying full-length on top of her.

Slowly she swiveled her head and met Violet's amused gaze.

"Well," the housekeeper said with a hint of smugness, "how nice to see you making the Yanks feel so much at home."

CHAPTER

✪ 13 ✪

Martin, as it turned out, was relatively unharmed, despite his spectacular backspring. Apparently, as the major explained, the kickback of the heavy gun had knocked the aged butler off his feet. Fortunately he had managed to imbibe a goodly portion of the expensive brandy Major Monroe had brought with him the night before, which explained his confusion as to the major's identity. The brandy had also relaxed him enough to survive the fall without any broken bones.

After examining him carefully, Dr. Sheridan pronounced the elderly man none the worse for wear, apart from a badly bruised shoulder and a considerable blow to his pride.

Much relieved, Elizabeth showed the doctor out then went back to the library to question Martin. "Where on earth did you get the gunpowder to load that thing?" she asked him as she helped him on with his coat.

"The master always kept a supply of it in the safe." Martin struggled to fasten his buttons. "He used to take the gun out sometimes to shoot it in the woods."

"Good heavens!" Elizabeth stared at him in amazement. "Did Mother know about that?"

"Of course not, madam." Martin found the dozen or so hairs on his head with his fingers and smoothed them in place. "This was strictly between us men. Women have no business around guns."

Elizabeth bristled at that but, under the circumstances, decided to let it go. "You could have killed the major," she said sternly. "I do not want you to ever touch that gun again."

Martin gave her a haughty look from under his brows. "It wasn't loaded," he said, managing to sound dignified in spite of his disheveled appearance.

"What do you mean it wasn't loaded?" Elizabeth folded her arms. "What on earth was all that noise, then? Not to mention the smoke."

Martin shook his head. "That was just the gunpowder going off. There wasn't any ammunition in the barrel. I put the gunpowder in when I heard about the invasion, ready for loading in case we were attacked." He frowned. "I'd forgotten it was in there. I just wanted to frighten the blighter, that was all. Take him captive until the police got here." He twisted his head to look around the room. "Where is he, anyway? Blighter hasn't escaped again, has he?"

"That man you attacked this evening was Major Monroe, one of the Americans billeted in our house. They are our guests. Martin, you really must remember these things. I can't have you running around attacking the Americans with a blunderbuss."

Martin flicked the dust off his jacket. "Excuse me, madam, but I was simply trying to protect you. If that had been a German officer, you would be thanking me for saving your life."

"No doubt," Elizabeth said dryly, "but right now I'm

thanking God you didn't kill Major Monroe and put us on the wrong side of this war."

She looked up as the door swung open and Violet hurried in. "How is he?" she asked anxiously.

"He'll live." Elizabeth sighed. "He was lucky this time."

"Silly old fool." Violet handed Martin a steaming mug of hot milk. "Here, drink this, then it's off to bed for you. The shock is enough to kill you."

Martin took the milk and sniffed. "Did you put brandy in it?"

"No, I did not." Violet wagged her finger at him. "You've had far too much as it is. Running around drunk with a blimmin' shotgun in your hands. Embarrassed us all, you did. You almost killed that nice major." She shot a look at Elizabeth. "Where'd he go, anyway?"

"Major Monroe took the decorations down to the town hall for me." Elizabeth glanced at the clock on the mantlepiece. "I should be getting down there. I told him to tell Rita I'd come down just as soon as the doctor left."

"Well, you'd better get on with it, then," Violet said, watching Martin gulp down his milk. "I'll see the old badger gets to bed all right."

Martin lowered his mug. His upper lip bore a white mustache of milk, which tended to deflate his dignity somewhat when he said pompously, "I am quite capable of getting myself to bed, thank you. If I wanted the services of a nursemaid, I'd hire a professional—someone much more youthful." His bleary-eyed gaze drifted down Violet's stick-like figure. "And with more bosom."

"Well, I never!" Violet looked outraged, though Elizabeth could swear she saw the housekeeper's lips twitch. "You wouldn't know what to do with a bosomy young woman if you had one, you mangy old goat. No more brandy for you, mister. It makes your tongue flap too much."

Martin raised his hand to his nose. "Where are my spectacles?"

"Here." Violet fished them out of her apron pocket. "They fell off while you were performing acrobatics out in the hall. Though I don't know why you bother to wear them. If you'd been looking through them properly you'd have recognized the major and wouldn't have taken a potshot at him. You're never going to see straight if you keep looking over the top of them."

Martin took the glasses and rather shakily strung them over his ears. "Has it ever occurred to you, Violet, that being unable to see clearly can sometimes be a blessing?"

Violet raised her chin, obviously taking the comment personally. "You're glad enough to see me when you're hungry, though, aren't you, you ungrateful old sod."

Elizabeth chose that moment to slip out, leaving the two of them to fight it out on their own. The frequent skirmishes between Martin and her housekeeper were harmless enough, and, although neither would admit it, disguised a genuine if grudging affection for each other.

They had been battling with each other for as long as Elizabeth could remember, from the good days when they'd been in charge of a houseful of servants, through the bad days when they'd watched the domestic staff gradually dwindle down to just the two of them.

Polly and Desmond, the gardener, had been hired less than two years ago, when His Majesty's service had claimed the resident gardener and the remaining maids had left to work in the military canteens. Martin and Violet were all Elizabeth had left now of her past life at the Manor House, and she loved them dearly. Even if they did drive her crazy now and again with their constant bickering.

Arriving at the town hall a short time later, Elizabeth found yet another form of chaos on her hands. Women appeared to be running hither and thither without any real design or destination. Rita Crumm stood on the stage, her face almost hidden behind the huge microphone, which apparently wasn't plugged in since not a word she spoke could be heard above the chattering of her crew.

Someone had draped an enormous Union Jack flag at the back of the stage, and Marge Gunther, easily the heaviest of Rita's followers, balanced precariously on a ladder while she attempted to hang a red, white, and blue garland over the window. Boxes lay all over the floor, while a nearby table was strewn with a tangled array of colorful paper decorations.

Elizabeth heaved a huge sigh, then stashed her handbag under her coat in the vestibule and rolled up her sleeves. It was going to be a long night.

The following morning Elizabeth rose with a strange sense of foreboding that she couldn't really pin down. The town hall had looked remarkably festive by the time she'd left, though not without a price. Tempers had been shortened and patience sorely tested, not to mention a strained muscle or two. All in all, however, she felt well satisfied with everyone's efforts.

All that remained now was to confer with Bessie and make sure the refreshments would be taken care of and the records and gramophone delivered on time. Ted Wilkins had dropped by during the decorating to assure her that a large supply of beer would be available for the dance. The major had promised to bring half a dozen bottles of Scotch and whatever else he could find, and so far everything seemed to be working out really well.

Even so, she couldn't quite dismiss the uneasiness that plagued her throughout breakfast.

She was thankful that Martin was unusually quiet, and even Violet seemed subdued.

"Tired," she explained when Elizabeth inquired about her well being. "I waited up until I heard you come in."

"Oh, you shouldn't have done that." Elizabeth looked at her in dismay. "I was perfectly all right."

"You had to ride that motorcycle past those woods in the dark." Violet rattled the dishes as she stacked them in the sink. "That German could still be loitering around there, waiting to jump out at you."

"I doubt it very much." Elizabeth glanced at Martin and was concerned to notice he looked unusually pale. "I'm quite sure he's left the area by now. The army personnel think so, too. They have called off the search."

"They can't do that!" Violet looked put out. "He killed that young girl. He's got to pay for it."

"*If* he killed her." Remembering the buttons, Elizabeth rose from her chair. "I'm going into town this morning. I was supposed to meet Polly in my office at half-past eight to show her how to do the filing. Please tell her I won't be back until eleven, so we'll have to do it then."

Violet looked disapproving. "I still think you're making a mistake letting that girl muck about in your office. Her head is too full of other things. She'll never pay attention long enough to learn anything, you mark my words."

"Well, we'll see." Elizabeth laid a hand on Martin's shoulder. "Are you feeling all right, Martin? You haven't said a word this morning."

Martin lifted his head, his eyes widening in surprise. "Good morning, madam! I didn't see you come in. I do beg your pardon." He started struggling out of his chair, and Elizabeth gently increased the pressure on his shoulder. "Don't get up, Martin. I'm just leaving."

"But you haven't had any breakfast yet, madam. You can't go out in this snowstorm with nothing in your stomach. Your mother will be most displeased. Has Geoffrey got the carriage ready yet? I told him the springs needed oiling. I do hope he saw to it."

Elizabeth exchanged a look with Violet, who rolled her eyes up at the ceiling. "Silly old fool's rambling again," she muttered. "Don't worry, Lizzie. You get on with what you have to do, and I'll take care of him."

"Perhaps we should have Dr. Sheridan take another look at him," Elizabeth said worriedly.

Violet made a hissing sound through her teeth. "If we sent for the doctor every time Martin got confused, the poor man would be here every day. You know how he gets. Give him an hour or two, and he'll be as good as new."

"He did take a rather nasty fall yesterday," Elizabeth said, unconvinced.

"I'll keep my eye on him," Violet promised. "Now get along or you won't be back in time to teach Droopy Drawers how to put papers in alphabetical order. That'll take you all day."

Wisely ignoring this piece of sarcasm, Elizabeth sent one last concerned glance at Martin, then left.

Roaring down the High Street a few minutes later, she returned the hand waves from the villagers, mostly women on their daily shopping trips. Heavy black clouds billowed across the steel-gray sky, forewarning a storm out at sea.

Elizabeth glanced up at the leaden sky and wondered if Major Monroe would be flying up there that day. How difficult it must be to find a bomb target when the clouds were so thick and low. The planes would have to fly beneath the clouds to find the target, which put them in dire danger of being hit by flack. Just the thought of it made her feel ill.

She shook off her inexplicable melancholy and coasted to a halt in front of Rosie Finnegan's clothes shop. Finnegan's Fashions had been a focal point of the High Street for the last century and a half, ever since Joe Finnegan had emigrated from Ireland, bringing his large family with him.

Their shop handed down from generation to generation, the Finnegan tailors had clothed the people of Sitting Marsh through the various fashion changes, from crinolines and corsets to short skirts and suspenders. Hemlines had gradually narrowed and risen over the years and now seemed to go up and down with every change of season. Through it all the Finnegans had treated their customers with courtesy and good old-fashioned Irish humor.

Rosie was no exception. Though quieter than many of her ancestors, she had a sense of dry humor that never let her down, even in the most trying times.

She greeted Elizabeth with a smile and a hot cup of tea laced with Irish whiskey—a treat that made a visit to Finnegan's worthwhile.

Sipping the potent brew from a thick china mug, Elizabeth listened to Rosie's account of the fight at the Tudor Arms. When she had finished, Elizabeth told her about the dance at the town hall.

"I'd appreciate it if you would put some notices up in your window about it," she said, looking around for somewhere to put down her mug.

Rosie took it out of her hand. "Be happy to, your ladyship. Bit of a short notice though, isn't it?"

"It is really, I suppose." Elizabeth leaned forward to finger a pale green silk gown hanging close by. Normally she bought all her clothes in London, staying overnight to give herself plenty of time to explore Harrods as well as the little boutiques in Oxford Street. Since the death of her parents, however, shopping in London had lost much of its charm.

"How much is this?" she murmured. The dress was a tad shorter than she was used to wearing, but she rather liked the flow of the skirt and the somewhat daring neckline was very flattering.

"It's rather expensive," Rosie said. "Five pounds, eleven shillings."

Elizabeth almost smiled. In the days when she'd had money, she'd thought nothing of spending five times that amount on a dress. Now she would have to think twice before splashing out on this one.

There was the dance tomorrow, of course. She hadn't been dancing since her marriage to Harry Compton.

Harry didn't like dancing. But then, Harry hadn't cared for any of her favorite pursuits. All Harry had worried about was which horse race to bet on, or which dog would win the Gold Cup.

It would be rather nice to go dancing again. And she hadn't bought anything in ages. "I'd like to try this on," she announced.

Rosie's eyebrows shot up. "Really? How wonderful! This will look absolutely gorgeous on you, m'm. I just know it." She showed Elizabeth into the minuscule dressing room and left her to try on the dress.

After removing her skirt and jumper, Elizabeth pulled the cool, slinky fabric over her head and let it fall into place. The shimmery green skirt clung to her hips, making her look at least five pounds slimmer. The color brought out the green in her hazel eyes. It was very definitely *her* dress. Just wait until Major Earl Monroe saw her in this little number.

The second the thought entered her head she was swamped with guilt. For a moment she was seized with an urge to tear off the dress and throw it in the corner where it couldn't tempt her anymore.

In the next instant she chided herself for being so juvenile. After all, she wasn't buying the dress for *him.* She'd had no intention of buying anything when she'd come to the shop. She had just as much right to buy a new dress as anyone else. Even if the money would be better spent on the gurgling water pipes.

Still arguing with herself, she slipped out of the gown and back into her sensible clothes. Then, with the dress draped over her arm, she walked back out into the shop, half afraid that the entire population of Sitting Marsh was waiting outside to sit in judgement of her.

Rosie was still alone, however, waiting for her with an expectant smile on her face. "How did it look, m'm?" she asked with an obvious and quite unsuccessful attempt not to seem too eager.

"Rather nice, actually." Shutting off the accusing

voice in her mind, Elizabeth handed over the gown. "I'll take it."

"That's wonderful. This will look so nice on you, m'm. Shall I have it sent up to the house?"

"No," Elizabeth said hastily. "I'll take it with me."

"Ah, going to wear it to the dance, m'm, are we? Very nice, too." Beaming, Rosie bore the creation away to be wrapped.

Elizabeth wandered around the shop while she waited, only half listening to Rosie's chatter from behind the counter.

"I don't normally carry such an expensive line in my shop," she said as she carried the package back to Elizabeth. "But I fell in love with this one. Would have liked it for myself, really, but I can't afford to pay that much for a dress."

She handed the package to Elizabeth, who took it from her as tenderly as if she were accepting a newborn baby. "Just put it on my account," she murmured automatically.

"Er—you don't have an account at Finnegan's, Lady Elizabeth." Rosie looked embarrassed. "But I'll open one for you right away, of course." She scurried back to the counter and began scribbling in a small ledger.

Feeling guilty again, Elizabeth waited for her to finish. She could hardly tell the woman that she didn't have enough cash to pay for the dress until the monthly rents were in.

When Rosie finally closed the ledger, Elizabeth handed her the buttons she'd been carrying in her pocket. "I was wondering if you've ever seen buttons like these before," she said casually. "They look as if they might come from a military uniform, though I don't recognize the emblem on them."

Rosie took the buttons and examined them. "They're not military buttons," she said at last. "The shanks are too fancy. I'd say they are more like blazer buttons, made to look as if they're military." She frowned, then added, "Wait a minute, m'm. I think I know where I might have seen buttons like these before."

She hurried out from behind the counter and crossed to the far wall, where a line of coats hung from a rack. "I've only just brought these out since the cooler weather came in a few weeks ago. They've been in storage since last winter, so I'm not sure but—" She broke off with a muttered explanation. "I thought so. Here." She pulled a navy blue reefer jacket off the rack and carried it over to Elizabeth. "See, m'm? They're identical."

"So they are," Elizabeth said slowly. "Have you sold many of these jackets lately?"

Rosie shook her head. "Not cold enough yet, is it, m'm. I've only sold two so far. One to Captain Carbunkle—he buys a new one every year—though I don't know why. I've known these things to last ten years or more."

Elizabeth lifted the sleeve of the thick, heavy wool garment. "And who bought the other one?"

"Sheila Macclesby. She was just in here day before yesterday. She told me Maurice had outgrown his old one, but if you ask me he probably lost it. That Maurice has never been right in the head. Makes me wonder how he ever gets the work done, now that Wally's not there. 'Course, the land girls help out a lot, I suppose, but I always say farming is men's work . . ."

Elizabeth nodded, listening with only half her mind. The other half was remembering the shiny buttons on the reefer jacket hanging in the cowshed and the blackened ones she'd dug out of the bonfire. There didn't seem any doubt now that the land girls had been right. It looked very much as if Maurice Macclesby had killed Amelia.

Had he had the presence of mind to hide his reefer jacket in the sacks to be burned? It seemed doubtful. More likely, his mother heard him arguing with Amelia that night and possibly discovered the body later. She could have seen the blood on Maurice's jacket and burned it to protect him.

Elizabeth thanked Rosie and left the shop, her mind still mulling over the possibilities. Sheila could also be the one who hid the body in the woods, hoping to place the blame for Amelia's death on the German. All possible, but how in the world was she going to prove it?

The evidence had been destroyed; the murder weapon—if the spade was, indeed, the murder weapon—had been throughly cleaned. The only witness to the murder would die herself before she incriminated her son. Elizabeth sighed. Once more it appeared that she was up against a solid brick wall.

CHAPTER

❦ 14 ❦

The next day passed in a flurry of activity as everyone worked together to prepare for the dance. Elizabeth had been quite pleased with Polly's work in the office the day before and decided to delegate some more duties. Thus leaving her more time to concentrate on the dance.

She'd tried to catch Major Monroe before he left that morning, in the hopes of finding out exactly what he planned to bring in the way of spirits, and was quite disappointed when informed by one of his officers that the major had left for the base in the early hours of the morning.

The significance of that disquieted her a great deal, and her thoughts kept returning to him throughout the day, despite her best efforts to put him out of her mind.

An hour before the dance was to begin, Polly had been dispensed to help Bessie deliver the gramophone and records. She arrived at Bessie's cottage to find her on her hands and knees in front of a small cabinet, doing her best to break it open with a dinner knife.

"It's locked," she explained when Polly crouched down beside her. "I can't find the key anywhere. I had it in that little blue egg cup on the mantelpiece, but it's not there now. All I can think is that the cat knocked it down, and it's rolled under the settee. It's too heavy to move on my own, but now you're here . . ."

She looked hopefully at Polly, who shook her head. "We don't have time for that now," she said briskly. "I've got a better idea."

She reached up to the knot of hair that Marlene had carefully piled up and pinned for her. Her fingers found a hairpin, and she drew it out carefully so as not to disturb the elaborate arrangement. Marlene would kill her if she messed up her hairdo now. She'd wanted a wave down the side of her face like Veronica Lake, but Marlene had talked her into wearing it on top of her head. She had to admit the style made her feel much older and more sophisticated.

In return she'd promised to tell everyone that Marlene had done her hair, so that her sister might get some new customers from North Horsham. There were bound to be girls coming to the dance from there, once the word got around. Word got around really fast in that town.

Realizing that Bessie was watching her with a worried expression, Polly grinned at her. "Watch this." She poked the hairpin into the keyhole, jiggled it around for a moment or two until she felt the lock release, then pulled out the pin. "Now try it."

Bessie's expression was skeptical as she twisted the handle, but it turned to amazement when the door opened easily. "How in the world did you do that?"

Polly shrugged. "A boy in school taught me. I kept losing the key to my desk, so he showed me how to open it with a hairpin. I got really good at it after doing it a few times."

"Well, it might be as well to keep that little talent to

yourself," Bessie warned as she drew out a pile of records. "Here, have a look through these."

Polly sat down on the carpet to examine the platters. "Crikey!" she exclaimed. "Look at all these. Benny Goodman, Louis Armstrong, Glenn Miller, Artie Shaw, Ted Heath, Duke Ellington . . ." She held one up in the air. "Frank Sinatra! My favorite! This is going to be a groovy dance. I can't wait to boogie-woogie with my Sam."

Bessie's eyes nearly popped out of her head. "What does all that mean?"

"It's jive talk." Polly went on sorting through the records. "The Yanks use it all the time."

"I always thought the Americans talked English." Bessie got up from her knees with a groan. "I'm beginning to think they talk a foreign language after all."

"I know. I have trouble understanding Sam sometimes. He comes from Tennessee and really slurs his words."

"Aren't you a bit young to be going out with Yanks?"

Polly scrambled to her feet. "I'm old enough. As old as most of them, anyway."

Bessie shook her head. "They're too young to be fighting in a war. It's criminal, that's what I call it."

Polly felt a stab of sympathy for Bessie. With her husband dead and both her boys fighting abroad, she must be feeling really lonely. Obeying an unexpected impulse, she put her arm around the woman's shoulders. "Tell you what, I'll introduce you to some of the Yanks tonight. They're all nice boys, and you could sort of mother them. They must be missing their mums as much as you miss your boys."

Bessie wiped a tear from her eye. "You're a good girl, Polly, and that's a fact." She beamed her familiar smile. "Come on, let's get these records over there so you can start dancing with your Sam."

"I just hope he gets there soon." Polly piled the platters into the shopping bag that Bessie held out to her.

"None of them had come back when I left." She couldn't voice aloud the thought that followed. *Please God, let him be all right.*

"You look very nice, madam," Martin announced when Elizabeth met him in the front hallway. "I hadn't realized you were going on the town. Shall I have Geoffrey bring around the horses?"

Elizabeth didn't have the heart to remind Martin that Geoffrey had died of tuberculosis many years ago. "That won't be necessary, thank you, Martin. I'll be using other transportation tonight."

Martin gave her a shrewd look. "Not that infernal machine that American drives around, I hope? It makes enough noise to wake the dead. I can't fathom for the life of me why they don't use their horses. I thought Americans rode horses everywhere."

"Only in certain parts of America, I believe." Elizabeth spoke automatically; her mind was elsewhere. It was well past eight o'clock, and so far there had been no sign of Major Monroe. She'd waited in the library in a fever of excitement, which had gradually diminished as the seconds had ticked by in that lonely room. Now she was beginning to get worried.

"You haven't seen any sign of the Americans this evening, have you?" she asked Martin. Perhaps she'd missed him somehow, and he'd gone on to the dance with his fellow officers.

"The American motorcars have not arrived back yet this evening," Martin said, glancing at the grandfather clock in the corner. "They are rather late, come to think of it."

Elizabeth suddenly felt cold. "Well, yes, I suppose I should be getting down to the town hall. If you see Major Monroe, please tell him I have already left and will meet him at the dance."

"Dashed ungentlemanly, if I might say so, ma'am. One does not abandon an appointment with a lady for any reason. Those Americans have a lot to learn about manners."

"I'm sure the major would have kept his appointment if he'd been able to do so," Elizabeth said quietly, "which is precisely what worries me." She headed for the door, trying to ignore the icicles forming in her stomach. "Don't wait up for me, Martin. Violet and I will probably be late."

Martin looked surprised. "I wasn't aware Violet was going to accompany you tonight, madam."

"She will be at the town hall, helping with the refreshments." Elizabeth peered at him over her shoulder. "Please don't do anything too strenuous tonight, Martin. I don't want you to hurt yourself when there is no one in the house to help you."

"I'll do my best not to hurt myself at any time, madam."

She smiled fondly at him. "Yes, well, you know what I mean."

"Wait a moment, madam. I'll get the door for you."

She waited for him to shuffle toward her, her gaze drifting past him to the stairs leading to the great hall. If only she could see the major's tall figure striding down those stairs. Impossible, of course, if the Jeeps hadn't arrived back. Still, it was hard not to hope for a miracle.

Martin finally reached the door and pulled it open. A gust of cool air greeted her as she stepped outside into the darkening evening. Soon the clocks would be turned back an hour, and the evenings would disappear altogether, swallowed up in the winter darkness that could fall as early as four in the afternoon. It was a depressing thought.

The depression weighed heavily on her shoulders as she climbed aboard her motorcycle. Fastening her head scarf more firmly under her chin, she braced herself for the cold ride to the town hall. In spite of the silver fox coat she wore, the wind from the sea would chill her bones. She could only hope that the town hall radiators were working properly and that the dance hall would be warm, though something told her she would not lose the chill over her heart until she saw the burly frame of Major Earl Monroe walking through the door to greet her.

"Look at this. Have you ever seen such a beautiful sight in all your life?" Marlene's voice was hushed in awe as she gazed around the crowded ballroom.

Polly followed her gaze. "Are you talking about the decorations or the men?"

Marlene grinned. "Both. Just look at those Yanks dance! Our boys can't dance like that."

"They're not even trying." Polly nodded at the walls lined with British soldiers, most of them with scowls on their faces. "They don't look very happy, do they?"

"I can see why. What with all the girls out there on the floor with the Yanks. Look, there's Lilly Crumm. Trust her to grab a Yank."

"I'm surprised her ma isn't out there with one, too." Polly gasped as she watched a tall, skinny American airman swing Lilly through his legs, then up over his back where she was suspended upside down for a heart-pounding second or two before being bounced back on her feet.

"No wonder they call it swing," Polly murmured. "Them Yanks are swinging the girls all over the place."

"So where is your Sam, then?" Marlene sent a searching glance around the room. "Can't see him anywhere."

Polly's stomach turned over. "He's not here yet. Must have been kept late at the base." She pretended not to notice Marlene's quick look of concern.

"He'll probably be here any minute."

"Yeah, I hope so." *He had to be there. It wouldn't be the same without him.* She'd got all dressed up for him and had put on the nylons he'd got her from the base. She just loved those nylons. She wouldn't have believed how silky and sheer stockings could be until she'd pulled on one of those filmy, almost transparent scraps of fabric over her legs. Just wearing them made her feel sort of slinky and ritzy.

She'd hitched up the skirt of her pink seersucker frock once she'd left the house and escaped from Ma's sharp eyes. She didn't really like the dress. It was too babyish. She'd wanted the black one hanging in Finnegan's big window, but Ma had put her foot down. Said it was too old for her.

At first she'd sworn never to wear the soppy pink thing. Then Marlene had shown her how to hitch up the skirt and pull the sweetheart neckline down lower, and it hadn't looked half bad after that. Though she still wished she could have had the black frock.

Idly she watched a good-looking Yank stroll over in her direction. Normally she'd have been all in a tizzy to see a man like that heading toward her. Funny how nobody seemed worth bothering about now that she had Sam. She sent another worried glance at the door. *Where the bloody hell was he?*

The dark-haired, dark-eyed Yank paused in front of her. She was all set to send him on his way with a polite refusal when he stepped past her and offered his hand to Marlene. "Wanna boogie?"

Marlene's face turned bright red. "I don't know if I can do it," she said nervously.

Polly gave her a mighty shove with her shoulder. " 'Course you can do it, silly. Just let him throw you about, that's all. He has to do all the work."

The American shot her a grin. "Thanks, babe." He grabbed Marlene's hand. "Come on, sugar, I'll show you how it's done." He charged onto the floor, dragging a protesting Marlene behind him.

Polly watched them for a while, forgetting her worries about Sam in the sheer enjoyment of watching her big sister make a proper fool of herself out there.

Marlene looked stiff and awkward as she tried her best

to keep up with the Yank, who seemed to be made of rubber the way he was twisting and twirling all around the floor. He spun her around a few times, until she looked really giddy, then grabbed her hands and swung her between his feet.

Polly caught her breath when Marlene, instead of hanging on to her partner's hands, let go instead. She skidded across the floor on her bottom and crashed into another couple. The girl was in midair at the time. Her partner caught her awkwardly, breaking her fall before they both landed in a heap on top of Marlene. Polly thought she was going to die from laughing.

Marlene's face was the color of a beetroot when she scrambled to her feet, tugging her skirt back down over her knees. She started to walk away from the Yank, but he pulled her back into his arms and started jitterbugging again all around the floor, with Marlene hanging on like grim death. Polly had to go and sit down before she wet her drawers laughing at her.

Half an hour later she wasn't laughing at all. By then Marlene had got the hang of the dancing and seemed to be having a really good time with her Yank, who hadn't left her side for a moment.

Polly sat staring at the door, fear looming like a cold dark cloud inside her. *Sam still hadn't come.* Although she'd fought hard against the thought, the unthinkable now seemed frighteningly possible. *Maybe this time Sam wasn't coming back at all.*

"These Cornish pasties are marvelous!" Elizabeth exclaimed after she'd bitten into the savory pastry. "What a treat."

Standing behind the refreshment table, Violet's face looked sour. "I could bake stuff like this if I didn't have to worry about rationing and that's all I had to do all day."

"I'm sure you could, Violet," Elizabeth hastened to reassure her. "Your trifle is beyond compare."

Violet's scowl vanished. "Well, thank you, Liz—"
She caught herself just in time and, after giving the
woman next to her a swift glance, added lamely, "Your
ladyship."

Nellie Smith seemed oblivious to anything except the
line of American airmen clamoring to buy the sandwiches and pastries piled up in front of her. Behind her,
one of Bessie's assistants stood frying fat, juicy sausages
over a camp stove, while a pan of fried onions sizzled
next to them. Elizabeth moved away from the enticing
aroma before she was tempted to sample the fat-laden
food.

The noise in the main hall was deafening. Captain
Carbunkle had turned up the volume to an ear-splitting
roar, and everyone on the dance floor yelled to be heard
above the blaring of trumpets and the pounding of
drums. Heads bobbed up and down, feet swung in the
air, hands were flung in every direction, and the vibra-
tion of stomping feet shook the floorboards.

Elizabeth, overwhelmed by all the raucous activity,
decided to get a breath of fresh air. On her way out she
scanned the floor, searching for a familiar square-cut
face with sun-bleached brown hair. Determined not to
give in to the fear that hovered inside her, she strode to
the main doors and pulled them open.

Cigarette smoke escaped above her head in a billow-
ing cloud. She took in several deep breaths of the cool,
fresh night air then closed the doors behind her, shutting
out the noise. With the ensuing silence came the terror
she'd tried so hard to ignore.

Something had happened to him. She was sure of that
now. It shouldn't hurt so much, but it did. She had no
right to feel this way about another woman's husband,
but sometimes a heart wouldn't listen to reason, and hers
seemed set on turning a deaf ear to common sense and
decency.

If she wasn't so miserable, she could laugh at herself
for being such a fool. After the fiasco of her marriage

to Harry, the very last thing she'd ever imagined doing was falling for another man. That would have been crazy enough. She hadn't been content with that. Oh, no, not Lady Elizabeth Hartleigh Compton. She'd had to break all the rules. She'd made the fatal mistake of falling for a man who was so far out of reach he might just as well be on the moon.

For a moment or two she allowed herself to wallow in self-pity. Then she pulled herself together. She was a Hartleigh, after all. Stiff upper lip and all that. Her attraction to Major Earl Monroe had been nothing more than an immature fascination for the unconventional, the inevitable lure of a uniform, and the appeal of a foreign lifestyle so different from her own. What woman hadn't been led astray by such enticements at some time or other in her life?

After all, what had she really lost? One couldn't lose that which one never had, and there were many thousands of women who had lost so much more. She had absolutely no right to go moping about feeling sorry for herself. Violet would be furious with her if she had any idea of her ridiculous and childish behavior.

Thus fortified, albeit with a heavy heart, Elizabeth squared her shoulders, shoved open the doors, and marched back into the thundering fray.

She noticed this time that the room had become sharply divided. On the one side, the Americans sat at the tables, either in groups or alone with a girl, while the rest of them jiggled around on the dance floor.

On the opposite side of the room, the British soldiers leaned against the wall, watching the dancing with bored expressions, or stood in groups muttering amongst each other.

It was those groups that worried Elizabeth the most. Even from that distance she could tell that the soldiers were not at all happy. A couple of them were making angry gestures and shaking their heads, while others scowled at the dancers on the floor.

It wasn't hard to understand why they were upset. With the exception of two or three women, all of whom looked old enough to be mothers of the uniformed men, the rest of the female assembly were either clinging to the arms of the Americans or flying over their backs.

It was time, Elizabeth decided, to get the two sides together before they were at each other's throats.

She headed for the stage, where Wally Carbunkle was busily sorting out records. "I think it's time for a break," she told him as she clambered up beside him. "See if you can find Priscilla. Tell her I need her to play the piano for a short while. I think I saw her over by the bar."

"I'll get her, your ladyship." Wally, looking very spiffy in a white shirt and red waistcoat, trotted off to find Priscilla.

Elizabeth stepped up to the microphone and looked down at the upturned faces of the dancers, most of whom looked disgruntled at being interrupted in their war dances. Undaunted, Elizabeth cleared her throat. "I think it's time we got everyone on the floor for a round of country dancing," she announced into the round, black mouth of the microphone.

Her words were met with a chorus of groans from the women, while the Americans looked at each other in confusion. A babble of voices arose from the floor while the women explained the art of English country dancing.

Sensing the lack of enthusiasm, Elizabeth tried again. "How about a Lambeth Walk?"

More mutters of explanation. The Americans merely looked horrified.

"Hands, Knees and Bumps a Daisy?"

This time the explanations were accompanied by half-hearted demonstrations from the abashed-looking women. Howls of laughter erupted from the men on the floor.

Elizabeth had to admit they did look rather ridiculous, slapping hands and bumping behinds. She made one last appeal. "All right, we'll play a slow song and make it a lady's invitation dance. Marlene Barnett, you start off by picking your partner, then when the music ceases, you each find another partner, and so on until everyone is dancing."

This announcement was met with a rumbling of grudging approval. Smelling victory, Elizabeth urgently beckoned to Wally Carbunkle, who was still hunting for Priscilla. He came back at a bumbling run and, panting for breath, climbed onto the stage.

"Don't you worry, Lady Elizabeth, I'll take care of it," he assured her.

She waited until the first strains of Frank Sinatra's clear, mellow voice filled the hall then thankfully left the stage. She'd done her best to integrate the crowd. Now she could only hope for the best.

Watching the dancers from the edge of the floor, she couldn't stop the ache growing in her heart. Couples danced cheek to cheek, shuffling around no more than an inch at a time. *Amazing,* she thought. She'd been fascinated by the way the Americans danced much livelier and faster than their British counterparts, and now they were dancing closer and much more slowly than she was used to seeing.

In fact, in view of the fact they were so closely entwined with their partners, the Americans' idea of a slow dance was quite sensual. *How marvelous it would have been to have danced with Earl Monroe that way.*

Even as she struggled to repress the thought, her attention was caught by a small disruption by the main doors. A group of American officers had entered, and Elizabeth was intrigued to see Polly Barnett rush up to one of them and throw her arms around his neck.

Then her heart seemed to stop when another of the officers broke away from the group and began walking unsteadily toward her. He was limping, she noticed, and he wore a piece of sticking plaster on his forehead. He

looked incredibly weary ... and unbelievably handsome.

He paused in front of her and held out his hand.
"Sorry I'm late. I believe this is our dance."

Speechless and embarrassingly close to tears, Elizabeth smiled up into the tired face of Major Earl Monroe.

CHAPTER

❈ 15 ❈

Suddenly the chattering and laughter in the ballroom seemed to ebb away as Elizabeth took Earl's hand, leaving only the soothing voice of Frank Sinatra to entice her onto the dance floor.

"You're limping," she said as he led her into the midst of the smooching couples.

"We had a little problem on the way back this morning."

"Won't it hurt you to dance?"

"I'll manage. Just don't ask me to jitterbug."

"Don't worry. I have no intention of breaking my neck for anyone." She glanced over to the group at the door. All of them appeared to have bandages of some kind, and one of them leaned on a cane. "What happened?"

"We caught some flak. Crippled the plane, but we

made it back close enough to land in a field. Took us a while to hitch a ride back to base."

Filled with concern, she looked up at him. His mouth was smiling, but the bleakness in his eyes frightened her. "That's a little problem?"

"We made it down in one piece. Better than ditching in the ocean."

"You shouldn't have bothered coming down here tonight. You must feel awful."

"I wouldn't have missed it for the world."

Her heart seemed to turn over. "I'm so glad you made it back." Such simple words that couldn't convey the gratitude she felt that he had been spared. This time.

"So am I." His gaze flicked over her. "Nice dress."

"Thank you." She had been right. Dancing this close with Earl Monroe was an interesting—no, captivating—experience. She felt quite light-headed.

She saw the other couples nuzzling each other and wanted so much to touch his cheek with hers. She had to remind herself sternly that he belonged to another woman. In an effort to reinforce that, she said deliberately, "Your wife will be very relieved to know you are safe."

His face was expressionless when he answered her. "Yeah, I guess so."

"Do you have children?"

"Two. Boy and a girl."

"They must all miss you very much. It's hard for children to be without their father."

"Yeah, well, they're almost grown up now. Brad's sixteen, and Marcia's a year older."

She looked at him in surprise. "You must have been very young when you had them."

"Right out of high school." He inclined his head in the direction of the stage. "Good music. Sinatra's a favorite of mine."

"Mine, too." Aware that he'd deliberately changed the

subject, she told him about the rest of Bessie's collection of records. Obviously it was painful for him to talk about his family. *He must miss them very much*, she thought, and chided herself for the deep pang of envy she felt.

The song ended much too soon, and she walked with him off the floor, wishing it could have gone on forever.

He said something to her, but the band music drowned out his words. She was about to ask him to repeat them when the sound of a disturbance over at the bar caught her attention.

A British soldier appeared to be arguing with an American, while a young woman attempted to get between them. Elizabeth recognized Lilly Crumm just as the soldier swung a punch at the other man's face. The American immediately retaliated and knocked the soldier to the ground.

It seemed to Elizabeth as if everyone in the room had been waiting for that moment. The tension had been building all night, and now all hell broke loose. Rita Crumm appeared from nowhere and dragged her daughter out of the way as British soldiers, American airmen, and too many women surged onto the floor. Fists began to fly, voices cursed, yelled, and screamed, while somewhere in the background someone was blowing on a whistle, barely heard above the racket.

Elizabeth signaled to Wally to turn off the music, since no one was listening to it anyway. Earl seemed to have disappeared, and she went up on her toes to scan the room for a sight of him. As she did so, a glass tankard sailed past her head, narrowly missing her. Someone bumped into her back, sending her forward into the flailing arms and kicking feet.

A painful blow on the shin made her cry out, and she twisted out of the way as a couple of men locked in mortal combat lurched past her. A pair of strong arms locked around her from behind, and terrified now, she struggled to release herself.

"Come on," Earl's voice said in her ear. "Let's get out of here."

Weak with relief, she let him guide her through the struggling bodies until they were at the edge of the crowd.

He put his mouth close to her ear again and asked, "Is there another way out of here?"

She pointed to a door tucked away in the corner behind the stage. Immediately he grabbed her hand and stumbled unevenly toward the door, dragging her behind him. They reached it safely, just as the shrill sound of whistles echoed throughout the ballroom.

"M.P.'s," Earl said, and pushed her through the door into the dark passageway beyond. "That will be trouble for the guys."

She didn't answer him until they were through the narrow passageway and out into the main foyer. Then she said with a sigh, "Well, that was a disaster."

He looked sympathetic. "I hate to say I told you so . . ."

"I know. Obviously this integration thing is going to take a lot more work. I'll simply have to come up with something else."

Inexplicably he gave a shout of laughter. "Lady Elizabeth," he said, still chuckling, "you are priceless! I like your spirit. Reminds me of the pioneers."

She would never know what prompted her to utter her next words. Maybe it was the approval in his eyes. Or the relief of seeing him back safe and sound from a near disaster. It could well have been all the excitement of being in the middle of a brawl. Or perhaps the two glasses of sherry she'd consumed while worrying about him. Whatever the cause, the words popped out of her mouth before she could stop them. "Please, Earl, do call me Lizzie."

Polly had been in the middle of the dance floor when the fight erupted. Sam had been wonderful, shielding her with his body as he swept her away from the brawling servicemen. She'd looked for Marlene but couldn't find her in all the confusion. Now she stood shivering outside the town hall, watching people stream down the steps.

"I hope she's all right," she told Sam. "Ma will never forgive me if something happens to her. We're supposed to watch out for each other."

Sam tightened his arm around her. "You can't be responsible for what she does. She's a big girl."

Polly looked at him in surprise. "Not that big. She's not as skinny as me but—" She broke off when Sam laughed.

"Not big in that way, though I guess she is built real nice, now that I think about it."

"Here, watch it!" Polly punched him in the arm. "Don't you go looking at my sister like that."

Sam dropped a kiss on her nose. "No need to worry, honey. I only have eyes for you." He started to sing softly, chasing away her doubts.

She couldn't stop worrying about Marlene, though, and kept her gaze fixed anxiously on the doors.

"She'll be okay," Sam said after a while. "She's almost your age. Not like she's a young kid or anything."

Polly felt a pang of guilt. What would he say if he knew she wasn't sixteen yet? She had to tell him some time. But not yet. Not until she knew for sure that he was well and truly hooked.

"I'm hungry," she said to take his mind off the subject of age. "Wish I'd had a couple of those bangers when I had the chance."

Sam stared at her. "Bangers?"

She grinned. "Bangers and fried onions. You know, sausages."

"Oh, you mean the hot dogs. They were swell!"

"Hot dogs? Is that what you call them?"

"Sure. Wiener in a bun. Everyone eats them at ball games. No fried onions—just relish and mustard."

She burst out laughing. "Don't say that around here,"

she said when she could breathe again. "People will think you're talking about something else."

"Say what?"

"Wiener." Again she exploded into laughter. "I can't tell you what it means. Just don't say it."

"Oh, I get it. Like when you say keep your pecker up."

She stopped laughing. "So what's wrong with that? It just means keep smiling, that's all."

Sam grinned. "Not where I come from."

"Really?" Polly frowned. "Looks like we talk a different language after all."

"You'd better believe it." Sam squeezed her shoulders. "Isn't that your sister coming down the steps now?"

"Yes, it is," Polly said in relief, then she gasped.

Marlene's normally immaculate hair was in a tangle all over her head, and one sleeve of her dress was torn. As she got closer, Polly could see an angry-looking scratch down one side of her face.

"What on earth happened to you?" she cried out as her sister reached her side.

The Yank with her, the one who'd been dancing with her all night, spoke first. "Eh, she's okay. Some prick took a swing at me, Marlene here jumped in, and his girlfriend tried to scratch her eyes out. Took two of us to pry 'em apart."

"I got the better of her," Marlene declared, though she looked ready to cry.

"We'd better get home," Polly said nervously. "Ma's going to be really upset when she sees that scratch on your face."

"It's too early to go home yet." Marlene's friend looked at his watch. "The night is still young. Let's go find a club where we can get a drink."

Polly laughed. "There aren't no clubs around here. Only the pub, and that shut at eleven."

"Eleven?" The Yank's black eyebrows rose in his

forehead. "What kind of time is that to close down? Don't they know there's a bunch of guys here looking for a drink?"

"I reckon you've all had enough to drink, Tony," Sam said, slapping the other man on the shoulder. "Why don't you take your girl home and call it a night?"

"Yeah, Tony," Marlene said, touching the ugly scratch with her fingers. "I want to go home now."

"Okay, sweetheart, anything you say." Tony winked at Polly. "See you later, babe." He slung an arm around Marlene's shoulders. "Where do we get a cab?"

Sam sighed. "This isn't New York, Tony. No cabs. You'll either have to take one of the Jeeps or hoof it."

Tony looked put out. "Okay, sugar, let's see if we can grab a Jeep before the rest of those bozos get out here." He looked at Sam. "You wanna come along with us?"

"Nope. Reckon we'll just mosey on along behind you."

"Okay. I'll wait after I drop Marlene off at the house and give you a ride back to base."

Sam grinned. "Take your time, buddy."

Tony's smile was wicked. "I plan to. See ya!"

Polly watched them leave, still feeling worried about Marlene. She seemed too quiet. Not at all like herself. "Do you know him?" she asked Sam as they started walking down the High Street.

"Who, Tony? Yeah, I guess I do. He's okay. Gets a little wild now and again, but he's a good guy. Your sis'll be okay with him."

"I hope so." She thought about it for a moment then said, "He's got a funny accent."

"He's a New Yorker."

"He talks too fast, and it's hard to understand what he's saying."

Sam laughed. "Most of the guys say the same about you gals."

"What? Don't you understand what I'm saying?"

"As long as I can see that look in those beautiful

brown eyes, I don't have to understand what you're say-ing."

She pretended not to understand him. "What look?"

He stopped and pulled her into his arms. Her heart melted when he gave her a long, lingering kiss. There was one thing about the Yanks, she thought happily as they continued on their way. They certainly knew how to make a girl feel good about herself. Even if they didn't really mean a word of it.

Elizabeth dreamed about Earl that night. It wasn't a good dream. It was vague and terrifying, filled with crashing planes and huge, leaping flames. She woke from it trembling and found it hard to go asleep after that. Part of her conscience insisted that the dream was her punishment for lusting after a married man. Not that she was really lusting after him, she hastened to correct herself.

She couldn't help the way she felt about him, but surely, as long as she didn't do anything about it, and never, ever let him know her feelings, what harm could there be in enjoying his company now and then?

None, she assured herself. He was a friend, that was all. Clinging to that faint ray of comfort, she finally fell asleep.

The telephone pealed its shrill summons the next morning while she was enjoying a boiled egg for breakfast with Violet and Martin in the kitchen.

Violet had been telling Martin about the fight at the town hall, and he was suitably horrified, insisting that the master would come down heavily on his head for not protecting the womenfolk from such barbaric behavior.

The fact that had he been at the dance the night before he might possibly have been trampled to death did not occur to him, and far be it for Elizabeth to point that out and diminish his role as protector.

She welcomed the ringing of the telephone as an effective diversion and waited for Violet to answer it. She watched the housekeeper's face and knew at once something momentous had happened.

Violet's replies were short and unrevealing, consisting mostly of "yes," "no," and "well I never."

Elizabeth waited impatiently for her to hang up the receiver. When she did, it seemed to take her forever to turn around.

"Well," she said finally, "you'll never guess what happened now."

"I'm sure I won't," Elizabeth said impatiently, "so why don't you just tell me?"

"That was George Dalrymple on the telephone." Violet's face took on a look of pure satisfaction. "He thought you'd like to know that the German is hiding in the old windmill out on Robbing Lane. Rita and her mob have the place surrounded. He's on his way out there now."

Elizabeth dropped her egg spoon with a clatter. "I must leave right away. It would be just like Rita to take matters into her own hands, and it will take George at least half an hour to get out there on his bicycle."

"You be careful, Lizzie," Violet warned. "You know how that Rita's lot gets when they're on the warpath. Never know what they'll be up to, that you don't. I don't want you getting hurt if they decide to go after that German."

"Save your worries for that poor boy." Elizabeth flung the words over her shoulder as she rushed from the room. Her beige wool coat hung on the hallstand, together with her black beret and scarf. She threw everything on, just as Martin came shuffling out into the hall.

"Madam, you can't fight the Germans empty-handed," he said as she headed for the door. "Take the blunderbuss with you. That will scare the pants off them!" He looked shocked. "Begging your pardon, madam. I can't imagine where I picked up that phrase."

"You've been listening at the keyhole to them Americans again," Violet said, hurrying down the hallway after him. "That's where you hear those things. Shame on you, Martin. You know what they say. Eavesdroppers hear no good of themselves."

"Well, that's as may be," Martin said haughtily, "but I can tell you that one hears no good of some other people, either."

Violet pulled up short. "What the blue blazes does that mean?"

"I'll be back as soon as I get things sorted out," Elizabeth said hurriedly, and before Martin had a chance to start his shuffle, she'd pulled the door open and closed it again behind her.

It took her only a few minutes to reach Robbing Lane on her motorcycle. She was glad of her scarf as the chill wind whipped at her face. It would soon be time to light the fires in the fireplaces. She could only hope they had enough coal to keep the fires going throughout the winter. December and January could be cruel months in Sitting Marsh, sometimes burying the village in deep snow for weeks at a time.

She wondered if bad weather would ground the Americans. If so, the officers would have a respite from their dangerous missions. In spite of her former fears, so far her uninvited guests had made little impression on day to day life at the manor. They left early in the mornings and didn't return until late in the evenings. Apparently they took all their meals at the base and generally kept to themselves.

If the bad weather grounded them, that could change. With time on their hands, the officers would become bored with sitting around the base or in their rooms in the east wing.

She couldn't help wondering if she'd see more of Earl Monroe. He'd seemed stunned when she'd blurted out those unfortunate words last night.

She should never have uttered them. She should have kept things on a formal level, so that there would be no hint of anything but an acquaintance between them. By allowing him to call her by her childhood name, she was putting their relationship on a much more personal level. Even though he didn't seem to realize that.

After his initial surprise, he'd acted pleased and flattered by her request. It was the very first time she'd called him by his first name, and it had seemed strange on her tongue. Even so, she had been unprepared for the impact of hearing her special name spoken in his deep voice. Never had it sounded quite so intimate.

She hastened to warn him never to call her Lizzie in front of anyone, and he'd promised to do so. He'd seemed amused by the warning and didn't seem to understand the significance. She hadn't bothered to explain. Better that he should think it simply a whim, rather than a breach of protocol that could lead to some serious gossiping among the villagers. After all, the more casual she kept this new arrangement, the better.

She couldn't help feeling, however, that she'd made a serious blunder in letting down her guard and that she would have to work very hard in order to ensure that it never happened again. That road could surely only lead to trouble and heartbreak.

CHAPTER

❧ 16 ❧

As Elizabeth rounded the curve on her motorcycle, she saw the group of women circling the dilapidated base of the old windmill. Rita stalked around, her strident voice too far distant to make out the words. The tone, however, was unmistakable. Rita was in her sergeant major mode.

Bracing herself for an inevitable confrontation, Elizabeth deliberately revved up the engine and roared onto the scene. Her spectacular skid halted her a few yards from where Joan Plumstone and Marge Gunther crouched behind a bush. They both leapt into the air when Elizabeth's wheels kicked up the dust behind them.

"Sorry," Elizabeth murmured as she cut the engine. "I didn't realize I was going so fast."

"Lady Elizabeth!"

The harsh voice made it sound more like a reprimand

than a greeting. Elizabeth grimaced as she watched Rita march toward her. "Good morning, Rita!" she called out. "Police Constable Dalrymple informed me that you have discovered the German pilot."

The mention of the constable's name appeared to take the wind out of Rita's sails somewhat. She spluttered for a moment then said testily, "There was no need for George to bother you, your ladyship. I'm quite sure my ladies can handle the situation."

Which was precisely why George alerted me, Elizabeth thought wryly. "Oh, I'm sure you can," she said, vigorously nodding her head. "I'm simply here to observe, that's all. In my role as lady of the manor, of course. I feel it's my duty to be on the scene when something of such significance is taking place."

Rather childish of her to remind Rita of her position, Elizabeth reflected, but necessary at times. Someone had to keep that woman under control.

"Well, as you can see, we have the entire place surrounded." Rita waved an arm to emphasize her statement. "He cannot escape now. In a moment I will give the word, and we will charge in there and get him. Isn't that right, ladies?"

A faint and definitely half-hearted chorus of "Right" answered her. Obviously the group of wary ladies did not share their leader's enthusiasm when it came down to actually tackling the poor boy.

"Might I strongly suggest that you wait until the constables arrive?" Elizabeth said firmly. "Even the most innocuous of animals can become vicious when cornered. I should hate to see any of you ladies hurt."

Several of the women began muttering in concern and were immediately silenced when Rita held up her hand. "We had planned on taking him by surprise, your ladyship. Since the noise from your motorcycle has now rendered that impossible, we shall have to resort to a charge. There are more than enough of us to overwhelm any attempt of the German to offer resistance."

Irritated now, Elizabeth climbed off her motorcycle and approached Rita. "I cannot allow you to do any such thing, Rita. Apart from the fact that the young man could be armed with a gun and could shoot you all on sight, you have no right to attack a human being unprovoked."

"Unprovoked?" Rita's voice rose shrilly in the cool air. "The man is a murderer! If you don't think that's enough reason to attack him"—she dropped her tone to acrimonious drawl—"*your ladyship*, then I have to respectfully question your sense of justice."

"You have no proof that this young pilot killed Amelia Brunswick." Elizabeth rashly went out on a limb. "In fact, evidence suggests that someone else was responsible for her murder."

Rita seemed taken aback. "Evidence? What evidence?"

"That's something you'll have to take up with P.C. Dalrymple. He should arrive at any minute, and until then I must insist that you not attempt to approach the windmill."

Several of the women muttered their agreement, apparently relieved the decision had been taken out of their hands.

Rita, however, became incensed with what she obviously considered mutiny. "All right, you miserable traitors!" she yelled. "You can all snivel on the sidelines if you like. But I'm not going to be called a coward. It's our duty to capture this bloody German, and we will disgrace ourselves if we turn away from our duty. So who's with me?"

She glared at poor Nellie, who, faced with choosing between the calm authority of the lady of the manor and the fevered rage of her fearless leader, sided with the person who could do her the most damage. "I'm with you," she quavered, raising a shaking hand.

Rita glared at a few other women, all of whom dragged themselves reluctantly over to stand behind her.

A dozen pair of eyes fastened on Elizabeth's face, pleading with her to stop Rita somehow.

Elizabeth opened her mouth to speak, but just then the door to the windmill opened a crack. It was enough to break the slim hold she had over Rita's intentions. With an inhuman howl, Rita pulled a wicked-looking knife from under her coat and brandished it in the air. "Come on, ladies! Tally ho!"

The crack closed immediately, but that didn't deter Rita. With her cohorts now hot on her heels, all feebly echoing that ridiculous war cry, she surged full tilt toward the windmill.

Elizabeth threw up her hands then determinedly gave chase.

Rita reached the door first. She shoved it open with her shoulder, raised the hand holding the knife above her head, and prepared to plunge inside.

Elizabeth briefly closed her eyes and prayed. When she opened them again, it seemed as if her prayer had been inexplicably answered. Rita appeared frozen in the doorway, while the group of women crowded silently behind her.

For a moment or two, Elizabeth was unable to move either. Whatever sight had met Rita's eyes, it was enough to stop the avenging woman dead in her tracks. Elizabeth couldn't imagine what could be dreadful enough to achieve that miracle, and right then she wasn't prepared to conjecture what Rita might have seen inside the windmill.

The shriek of rage shook her out of her stupor. The agonized sound had come from Rita, who had now disappeared inside the dark depths of the rotting building.

Galvanized into action, Elizabeth pounded forward as fast as her sensible shoes would allow. She skidded to a stop when she reached the silent group and thrust her way past them to the door. Peering inside, she half expected to see Rita dead on the floor. The sight that met her eyes, however, shocked her to the core.

Rita stood immobile, apparently staring into the dark shadows in front of her. Elizabeth could just make out the two figures inside. One was the German pilot, his back pressed up to the wall. Standing protectively in front of him, a half-eaten loaf of bread in her hand, defiance in every line of her young body, was Lilly Crumm.

"Apparently Lilly had been feeding him for the past two or three days," Elizabeth told Violet when she returned to the Manor House later. "Her mother had no idea, of course. She was totally flabbergasted. She was all set to tear the poor boy apart with her bare hands. Luckily, George and Sid arrived to take him into custody before anyone could do him any damage."

Violet looked up from the stove, where a pot of soup sat bubbling. "Lord knows what Rita Crumm will get up to next, but mind you, she's got her hands full with that Lilly."

"Like mother, like daughter, I'm afraid." Elizabeth dropped her handbag on the table and sank onto a chair. "They are both very strong-willed women."

"Well, I know someone else like that." Violet coughed and hurried on before Elizabeth could protest. "Anyway, I'm so glad they caught that German. Now we don't have to worry about a murderer running around the woods, and everything can get back to normal. Polly can go back to riding her bicycle home instead of bothering that nice American officer."

"I'm not so sure about that," Elizabeth murmured.

"Well, I'll make sure she doesn't bother him," Violet said, giving the soup a vicious stir with her wooden spoon.

"No, I mean that we don't have to worry about a murderer running loose."

Violet gave her a sharp look. "How's that? George and Sid are going to keep him a prisoner, aren't they? They're not going to turn him loose? After all, he is a

German bomber pilot. The same kind who dropped the bomb on London that killed your parents, remember?"

Elizabeth gave her a wry look. "I'm not likely to forget that. And no, they won't turn him loose. In fact, the last I heard, George was telling everyone that the prisoner would be hung for murder. What I meant was, I don't think he killed Amelia Brunswick."

"Then who did?"

Elizabeth met Violet's curious gaze. "I'm pretty sure I know, but I can't prove it. I really don't want to say anything until I'm certain I'm right. At this point I'm afraid it's all conjecture."

Obviously disappointed, Violet shrugged. "Well, if you feel like that."

"The thing is," Elizabeth said slowly, "I keep getting the feeling that I know how to prove it. I just can't quite pull it out into the open."

Violet's eyes narrowed with interest. "Something you saw, perhaps?"

Elizabeth thought about it. "No. It's more like something someone said, I think. Darn, I wish I could remember."

"Stop trying. It will come to you in a flash, you'll see. Happens to me all the time. I wake up in the night sometimes shouting the answer. Good job I never married. I'd scare a husband to death."

Elizabeth nodded. "I suppose you're right. Thinking so hard about it makes my head ache anyway." She sniffed the air. "The soup smells good."

"Oxtail. Lucky to get it. Jack Mitchem didn't have much in the shop today—just some scrawny-looking chickens and some fatty pork. Maybe you could ask your Major Monroe if he can bring us some more steak."

"He's not my major," Elizabeth muttered, relieved that Violet couldn't see the way her heart jumped at the mention of his name.

"You never did tell me why he's wearing a bandage on his head."

"His plane went down in a field, and they had to get a lift back to base."

"Oh, my!" Violet clutched her throat. "Poor man. What about the rest of them? Are they all right?"

"Just bruises and cuts, Earl said." His name had slipped out without her thinking.

She saw Violet's eyes widen with understanding. "Earl now, is it," she said softly.

Elizabeth sighed. "I decided it was time to join the modern world, that's all. Everyone seems to be on a first-name basis nowadays. Must be the war, I suppose."

"The war changes a lot of things." Violet tilted her head to one side. "I just hope you know what you're doing, Lizzie."

"I'm not doing anything, so you can stop looking at me like that." Elizabeth sought to change the subject. "I left Polly to finish entering the notes from the council meeting into the ledger. Do you know if she finished them?"

Violet looked frustrated at being robbed of what promised to be an interesting conversation. "I don't know if she finished them or not. The last I saw of her she was looking for the vacuum cleaner. Said she'd lost it. How can you lose a vacuum cleaner, I ask you?"

"It isn't lost," Elizabeth murmured, only half paying attention. "I saw it standing at the end of the great hall last night, so I put it back under the stairs where it belongs."

Violet sniffed. "Well, isn't that just like that young lady. The last place Polly would ever think of looking for something is the very place where it should be."

Elizabeth stared at her. "That's it," she said at last. "Violet, how long will it be until the soup is ready? I have an important visit to make, and I need to do it as soon as possible."

An hour later Elizabeth arrived at the Macclesby farm.

Maisie hailed her as she crossed the yard to the farmhouse.

Elizabeth returned the greeting. "Is Mrs. Macclesby in the farmhouse?" she asked as Maisie turned away.

"No, your ladyship." Maisie hooked a thumb in the direction of the cowsheds. "She's in there, shredding up mangolds. Kitty was supposed to do it, but she took sick. Something she ate, I think."

"Oh, I'm sorry. I hope she soon feels better." Elizabeth hurried over to the sheds, where she could hear the sound of the hopper. Inside one of them she found Sheila, busily turning the handle of the large wooden box, while the beets bounced and rattled around before the blades shredded them to pulp.

Sheila looked surprised to see her and immediately let go of the handle, brushing her hands down her stained apron. "Lady Elizabeth! You always seem to catch me when I'm looking my worst. Can I offer you a cup of tea or cocoa?"

Elizabeth shook her head. "I don't want to interrupt your work."

"Oh, don't worry about that." Sheila waved a hand at the hopper. "It's almost done, and one of the girls can finish it off later. I don't want you standing around a drafty old shed. It's getting really cold out there. Come inside, and I'll make a nice cup of tea."

Elizabeth followed the farmer's wife into the house and accepted a seat on the armchair Sheila offered her. "Please, don't bother with the tea just now," she assured her. "There's something rather important I want to talk to you about."

Sheila's face immediately turned wary, and she sat down on the edge of the settee, twisting her hands in her apron. "What about, your ladyship? No trouble, I hope?"

Elizabeth sighed. "Sheila, the first day I was here, after Amelia's body was discovered in the woods, Maisie told you she'd left a spade outside the night before, and when she'd gone to retrieve it the next morning, the spade had vanished."

Sheila violently shook her head. "I don't remember—"

"You told her it was back in the shed where it belonged," Elizabeth continued. "Later on that day Maisie thanked you for cleaning the spade for her. You denied doing so."

"Did I? I can't recall—"

"The medical examiner believes that the killer might have used a spade to kill Amelia. A spade that was probably left out overnight . . ."—she deliberately paused—"and later cleaned."

Sheila's hand closed over her throat. "So that's how that German killed that girl. He used one of my spades and cleaned it off afterwards—the murdering sod. Beg your pardon, m'm."

"That's quite all right." Elizabeth looked down at her gloved hands. "There's just one thing I don't understand. You said you heard Amelia arguing beneath your window, but you decided not to go down to investigate."

"That's right, your ladyship. How glad I am now that I didn't. I could have walked right into a murder and been struck down myself. Lucky escape, that's what I had." Sheila started fanning herself with the skirt of her apron.

"If I remember, you told me you hadn't been out of the house the next morning when I arrived. Yet you knew that the spade that had been left out overnight had been put back in its proper place in the shed. How could you have known the spade was back in the shed, unless you saw it there after Amelia was killed?"

Sheila appeared to have no answer to that question. She sat as if turned to stone, staring at Elizabeth without a flicker of expression in her eyes.

"I'm sorry, Sheila," Elizabeth said gently. "I think you heard Amelia arguing with your son right under your window that night. By the time you got down there, it was too late. He'd killed her. You took the body into the woods and hid it, hoping to put the blame for her death on the German pilot. Then you cleaned off the spade, put it back in the shed, and later burned Maurice's bloodstained reefer jacket."

Sheila's voice sounded strangled when she spoke. "I don't know what you're talking about," she said hoarsely. "My son isn't capable of killing anyone. You know that. He wouldn't hurt a fly. He liked Amelia— he would never have hurt her."

"He probably didn't mean to," Elizabeth said, her heart aching for the poor woman. "Maybe Amelia was teasing him, and he just wanted her to stop. People whose minds have not fully developed are not capable of reasoning like normal people. Maurice was just trying to defend himself."

"He would never have hurt her. Never."

Elizabeth leaned forward and patted the trembling hands. "Sheila, you know I have to tell the constables. There's no guarantee that something like this won't happen again. I came to you first, because I wanted to give you the chance to prepare Maurice for what will happen to him. I'm quite sure, given the circumstances, that he won't be put in prison. The jury will most likely find him insane, and he'll be sent to an asylum where he can be watched and protected for his own sake. You'll be able to visit him—"

"No!" The words were wrung from Sheila's lips. She leapt to her feet and walked over to the window, where she stared out at the shadows creeping across the farm-yard. "Maurice didn't kill Amelia," she said bleakly.

"Sheila—" Elizabeth rose just as the farmer's wife turned to face her.

"My son did not kill that woman." Her voice was stronger now, with a note of defiance. "I did."

CHAPTER

❈ 17 ❈

Elizabeth stared at the white-faced woman, unable to comprehend what she'd just heard. The possibility that Sheila Macclesby had committed murder had never occurred to her. "Why?" she asked at last.

Sheila came back to the settee and sat down. She had lost all her defiance now and looked unspeakably tired. "Maurice was . . . fond of Amelia. He followed her around like a little lost sheep, practically begging her to notice him. She either ignored him or shouted abuse at him." Sheila shivered. "How I hated that girl. She was so cruel."

She sat staring down at her hands for several seconds. When she looked up again, tears glistened in her eyes. "Lady Elizabeth, do you have any idea what it's like to watch your son being constantly tormented and bullied? All through his school years, my Maurice had to put up with it. I'd find him sitting on the front doorstep, crying his heart out because he couldn't understand why all the other kids hated him. I tried to explain that he was different, and that made him special. That the other kids just didn't understand him, that was all." She shook her head. "I could tell I wasn't getting through to him."

Elizabeth swallowed past the lump in her throat. "It must have been difficult for both of you."

"Difficult?" Sheila lifted her hands and let them drop in her lap again. "It was heartbreaking, m'm. That's what it was." She paused for several more painful seconds before continuing. "I thought that once he left school and I could keep him here on the farm with me, that it would all be over. That nobody would ever torment Maurice again. But then Amelia came, with her blond hair and her blue eyes and that soft laugh of hers—as soon as my Maurice set eyes on her, he was smitten. I could tell."

"So he followed her around."

"Yes." Sheila sighed. "I tried to stop it, of course, but the more I tried, the more determined he got. I'd never seen Maurice like that. . . . It frightened me. I knew there would be trouble."

"So it *was* Maurice you heard arguing with Amelia that night."

Sheila nodded. "He must have been waiting for her to come home. As soon as I heard them I rushed downstairs and out the door. I heard her as I came around the corner. She was yelling at him. Terrible things." Sheila shuddered. "She called him filthy names, told him he was never to come anywhere near her again. Told him he wasn't fit to be around girls. I won't repeat everything she said to him, but I could see what it was doing to him. When I got to him, he was crying. Big tears just rolled down his face."

The silence in the room grew more ominous as Sheila relived the memory of that night. Elizabeth could hear her own heartbeat thudding in her ears. Part of her ached with sympathy for the mother who'd had to watch her son suffer so much. Yet she couldn't condone the murder of a young woman, no matter how provoked.

"When I saw my son cowering like a beaten puppy," Sheila said, her voice cracking with the effort to speak, "something inside my head seemed to snap. I just couldn't take it anymore. The spade was leaning against the wall. I picked it up and I smashed it into that cruel, cruel face." She raised her hands and covered her face. "I didn't mean to kill her. I just wanted to shut her up. But the spade slipped in my hands, turned sideways and sliced into her head. As soon as she went down, I knew she was dead." She began to cry—softly, like a baby kitten mewing for food.

Elizabeth waited until the pitiful sound stopped then asked gently, "So you took the body to the woods?"

Sheila nodded and wiped her eyes with a large handkerchief she'd taken from her apron pocket. "When Amelia fell to the ground, Maurice held her in his arms. He was crying so hard I felt sure he'd wake everyone up. His coat was soaked in blood, and I knew I'd have to get rid of it. I took it off him and made him go to bed. Then I put Amelia into the wagon, hitched up Daisy, and went to the woods."

"And you burned Maurice's jacket."

Sheila nodded. "I'd already told the girls to burn the sacks. I put the jacket inside one of them, then I went and bought him a new one." Her face crumpled again. "I don't think he'll ever forgive me for what I did."

Elizabeth reached out a hand, then drew it back. "I'm sure he will," she said. "In time."

Sheila let out her breath in a long sigh. "What happens now?"

"I'll have to notify the constables." Elizabeth rose. "I'm sorry, Sheila. If there was any other way—"

"No, Lady Elizabeth. I know I have to accept my punishment for what I did. It's Maurice I'm worried about. Who's going to take care of him?"

"I'll see what I can arrange." Elizabeth paused at the

door. "Try not to worry about Maurice. You have to think of yourself now."

Sheila's smile was filled with sadness. "I'll always worry about him. He's a good boy. He can't help being different."

It was with the greatest reluctance that Elizabeth paid a visit to the constabulary. George and Sid were shocked, and although they tried hard not to show it, suitably impressed that Elizabeth had uncovered the real murderer.

"I don't know how you worked that one out, your ladyship." George smoothed a hand over his bald head, a sure sign that he was embarrassed at having accused the wrong man. "Much less have her confess the whole story."

"There really wasn't much else she could do once I presented her with the evidence," Elizabeth said modestly. "I think she was mostly concerned that Maurice might be blamed."

"Well, m'm, Sid and I certainly appreciate your efforts in this matter." He raised a warning finger. "I must advise you, however, that it is not a good idea to go poking around where a murder has been committed. You could very well get yourself into hot water that way." He glanced self-consciously at Sid, as if suddenly realizing whom he was lecturing. "If you'll excuse me, your ladyship. It's just that we wouldn't want anything happening to our lady of the manor, now would we, Sid?"

"Oh, no, George. Can't have that." Sid beamed at Elizabeth. "Don't know what we'd do without you, m'm."

"Well, that's very reassuring to hear." Well pleased with herself, Elizabeth got up from her chair. "One thing I do want to impress upon both of you. I promised Sheila I would make arrangements for someone to look after Maurice. I want to be sure that's taken care of before you arrest her."

George nodded. "Don't you worry about that, m'm. Under the circumstances, I wouldn't be at all surprised if Wally was sent home to take care of his son until something better can be arranged."

"That would be a big help. I'll see if I can pull a few strings in Whitehall."

"Appreciate it, m'm." George hurried across the room to open the door for her. "Thank you again for your help."

"Not at all. I'm not happy to see Sheila Macclesby go to prison, but I wouldn't want to see anyone pay for a crime he didn't commit."

George looked embarrassed again. "No, m'm. Neither would I."

Violet plied her with questions when Elizabeth returned to the manor. "What made you think of that spade being put back in the shed?" she asked after Elizabeth had told her the whole story.

"It was when you told me about the vacuum cleaner." Elizabeth put her teacup down on its saucer and leaned her elbows on the kitchen table. "You said that the last place Polly would look is where something should be. I remembered Sheila telling Maisie the same thing. That's when I realized that if she was telling the truth about that night, she couldn't have known the spade was back in the shed. She said she didn't go down after she heard Amelia arguing, which meant, of course, that Amelia was still alive at that point."

"And when you went over the next morning, she said she hadn't been out of the house."

"Exactly. So the only way she could have known about the spade was if she put it back in the shed herself or saw who did. Then again, if she'd seen the German pilot put it back there, why would she lie? It seemed obvious that she was covering up for someone, and that could only have been Maurice."

"You never thought it might have been her who killed Amelia?"

"Not for a moment," Elizabeth admitted.

Violet opened the oven door and drew out a cherry pie that looked as delicious as it smelled. She carried it over to the windowsill and sat it down in front of the open window to cool.   "Do you think she really did it, or is she still covering up for her son?"

Elizabeth sighed. "I asked myself that question a dozen times on the way to the police station. There's no question that Maurice loved Amelia in his own way. I've seen him with the creatures he's cared for, and I really don't think he has the temperament or the emotional strength to hurt someone he loved. Then again, I could well be wrong. I suppose it's up to the jury to decide."

"Well, all I can say is, I don't envy them their job."

Elizabeth met her gaze. "And neither do I."

Later that evening, unusually restless, Elizabeth decided to take a short walk around the grounds to clear her head. Soon it would be too cold for her nightly strolls, which had become rather rare of late. Before her marriage she had often joined her parents on their nightly habit of walking the grounds, but now that she was alone she didn't care to be out there after dark.

There were just a few days left now before the daylight savings time ended, and already the dusk had darkened into night shadows among the trees. Her mind dwelling heavily on the tragedy she had seen unfold, she started violently when a shadow detached itself from a thick grove of beech trees and moved toward her.

For an instant her heart stopped beating then resumed at a rapid pace when she recognized the chunky frame of Major Earl Monroe. She hadn't seen him since that ridiculous moment when she'd blurted out her permission for him to call her Lizzie. She didn't quite know how to face him now. She could only pray she hadn't given anything away in her foolishness.

To her relief, he greeted her as he always did, with just the right amount of respect in his voice. "Evening, ma'am. Mind if I join you for a minute or two?"

Adversely, and quite ridiculously, she was shattered that he hadn't used her pet name after all. "Good evening, Major. I wasn't expecting to see you out here. How's the leg?"

Moonlight spilled across the lawn, illuminating his handsome face. Behind him the Manor House rose dark and still, its windows hidden by the blackout blinds. As she waited for him to answer, somewhere deep in the woods she heard an owl hoot a warning.

"It's doing a lot better, thanks." He moved closer, and she noticed his limp was less pronounced tonight.

"I'm glad. And the others?"

"All recovering nicely."

"I'm happy to hear it." Her heartbeat slowed in disappointment. They were talking to each other like strangers. What had happened to the easy companionship she had so enjoyed in recent weeks? Had she spoiled everything by that ridiculous outburst last night? Her heart ached with regret.

He continued to watch her as if expecting her to say something else. She cast about for a topic and came up with the one uppermost in her mind. "I don't know if you heard, but we have discovered who killed Amelia Brunswick."

He nodded. "The farmer's wife. I heard."

"Ah."

"I also heard you were responsible for her being arrested."

She shrugged. "I just happened to be in the right place at the right time."

"And what's this I hear about you fighting off a horde of angry housewives to save the German kid from being lynched?"

She had to smile at that. "This isn't the Wild West, Major. Rita and her ladies were merely doing what they thought was their duty. I simply appealed to their better judgement."

His gaze remained watchful on her face. A sudden breeze lifted a lock of his hair and drifted it across his forehead. He seemed not to notice. "Are you always this modest?"

She didn't know how to answer that. While she was still searching for something sensible to say, he took her breath away with his next words.

"I got the impression that you kind of regretted asking me to call you Lizzie last night. I just want you to know that I won't be offended if you want to take it back." He shoved his hands in his trouser pockets. "I can't pretend to understand all this protocol stuff over here, but I know enough to want not to tread on anyone's toes."

She had to swallow at least three times before she could answer him. "Major . . . I mean, Earl, I want you to understand something. I know I've told you most of this before, but it bears repeating. As you know, there have been generations of Lord Hartleighs overseeing the village of Sitting Marsh. When my parents died two years ago, for the very first time the villagers' guardian had become a woman. As I've already told you, I had to work very hard to gain the trust and respect of my tenants. I had to prove myself over and over again. I'm still proving myself. I can never let down my guard for a moment, because there are still some people who consider this job too important to be entrusted to a woman."

"From what I've heard, the people of Sitting Marsh worship the ground you walk on. I've heard some of them defend you when one of my guys questions your position in the village. They can't say enough good things about you."

In spite of herself, Elizabeth glowed with the praise. "Well, that's very gratifying, but I must never forget to uphold the traditions and the principles that have been set by my family over the years. My mother was an outsider, and they never let her forget it. The fact that they accept her daughter at all is a miracle. No matter what my personal beliefs or needs might entail, I will always, always put my people first."

He nodded, looking grave. "In other words, no Lizzie."

She hesitated for a long moment. "Perhaps you'd settle for just Elizabeth, as long as it's strictly between us, of course?"

"If you'll agree to call me Earl. As long as it's strictly between us, of course."

He'd mimicked her British accent with his last words, and she laughed. In her best American accent, she drawled, "Earl, you gotta deal."

He held out his hand. "Is it permissible to shake the hand of a lady of the manor?"

"Well, in the old days we were more used to our hands being kissed, but I'll settle for a handshake."

She clasped his hand and was enchanted when he raised it to his lips. It would be morning, she vowed, before she washed that hand again.

"I have a surprise for you," he said when he let her hand go. "It's in my room. How about I go get it and meet you in the library in, say, ten minutes?"

Intrigued, she nodded. "Ten minutes."

She walked with him back to the house, where he left her to go in through the back door leading to the east wing. She entered by the front door and made her way to the library, where she waited in a fever of curiosity as to what the surprise might be.

When he finally entered the room, he was carrying a large basket. She watched in astonishment as he laid the wicker container on the floor then opened the lid.

The gasp that left her lips was both shock and delight when two furry heads popped up and gazed at her with sleepy brown eyes. With a cry she dropped on her knees beside them. "Oh, they are so beautiful. Where did you get them?"

"One of the guys on base was talking about his girl-friend trying to get rid of some pups. I remembered you said you were thinking about getting a couple of dogs. I took a look at them and decided you all belonged to-gether."

She laughed as the puppies spilled out of the basket and started exploring. "Just look at their feet—they're huge! What kind of dogs are they?"

"Best we can tell, they're a bloodhound mix." He looked worried. "I just brought them for you to take a look. If you don't want them I'll take them right back."

She watched the two roly-poly, cumbersome puppies stumbling over each other in their eagerness to sniff around the potted palm in the corner. The words that came immediately to mind were *double trouble*. Life would become a little more complicated with these new arrivals in the household. Earl had given them to her, however, and nothing on this earth could tear them away from her. "We'll have to come up with some good names for them."

"How about George and Gracie?"

She raised her eyebrows at him.

"It's from a television show back in the states—'Burns and Allen.' George and Gracie are the stars."

She smiled at him. "I like that. George and Gracie it is."

"Good choice." He smiled back, and her happiness was complete.

MARGARET COEL

THE EAGLE CATCHER

When Arapaho tribal chairman Harvey Castle is found murdered, the evidence points to his own nephew. But Father John O'Malley doesn't believe the young man is a killer. And in his quest for truth, O'Malley gets a rare glimpse into the Arapaho life few outsiders ever see—and a crime fewer could imagine...

❏ 0-425-15463-7/$6.50

THE GHOST WALKER

Father John O'Malley comes across a corpse lying in a ditch beside the highway. When he returns with the police, it is gone. Together, an Arapaho lawyer and Father John must draw upon ancient Arapaho traditions to stop a killer, explain the inexplicable, and put a ghost to rest...

❏ 0-425-15961-2/$6.50

THE DREAM STALKER

Father John O'Malley and Arapaho attorney Vicky Holden return to face a brutal crime of greed, false promises, and shattered dreams...

❏ 0-425-16533-7/$6.50

THE STORY TELLER

When the Arapaho storyteller discovers that a sacred tribal artifact is missing from a local museum, Holden and O'Malley begin a deadly search for the sacred treasure.

❏ 0-425-17025-X/$6.50

EARLENE FOWLER

introduces Benni Harper, curator of San Celina's folk
art museum and amateur sleuth